"The ....n."

His meaning ....ip with this man would be a dream come true. But once Wyatt learned the truth, he'd want nothing more to do with her.

"Leigh? Have I misread some signals?"

She forced herself to meet his gaze. She remembered those eyes blazing down at her in the lamplight of her bedroom as he filled her with his heat.

She shook her head, willing herself to be as honest as she dared. "You haven't misread anything, Wyatt. I'd welcome more time together if we could find it. But things are a bit...overwhelming right now."

"Fine. For now...but not for long, Leigh. As you know, I'm not a patient man." Tilting her chin with a finger, he brushed a feathery kiss across her lips.

She ached with wanting him—his arms around her, his skin naked against hers. But was she willing to risk the consequences?

* * *

The Nanny's Secret
is part of the #1 bestselling series
from Harlequin Desire—
Billionaires and Babies: Powerful men...
wrapped around their babies' little fingers.

* * *

If you're on Twitter,
tell us what you think of Harlequin Desire!
#harlequindesire

Dear Reader,

As I sit down to write this, bells are ringing in England to herald the birth of a new little prince. However you may feel about the royal family, a sweet, healthy baby is always something to celebrate.

Most babies aren't born princes and princesses—except to the people who love them. But there's something about a new baby that inspires love and hope. The first time that tiny hand reaches up to clasp your finger, you lose your heart.

My own firstborn son arrived a few days before Christmas. He's grown now, but I still remember the joy of bringing him home and the wonder of holding him in my arms. He was so small and needy. And as a new mother, I was so scared.

Not every baby is born under ideal conditions. That's what this story is about. Little Mikey enters this world as the result of a teenage blunder. His unmarried sixteen-year-old mother loves him and wants to keep him, but she's still a child herself. His billionaire grandfather, still young, virile and handsome, has no idea how to cope with a willful teenage girl and her newborn son, who his ex-wife literally dumped on his doorstep.

Enter an unlikely nanny, challenged with helping these three become a family. Mary Poppins she isn't. But her devotion to little Mikey and her determination to give him a good start in life go far beyond what might be expected of hired help.

Mikey's sexy grandfather begins to see her as more than a nanny...much more. But the beautiful Miss Leigh Foster is not what she seems. The secret she hides is powerful enough to turn all their lives upside down.

This story was written as a celebration of babies and mothers everywhere. If it touches you, I would love to hear. You can contact me through my website, www.elizabethlaneauthor.com.

Happy reading,

Elizabeth

THE NANNY'S SECRET

ELIZABETH LANE

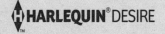

HARLEQUIN® DESIRE

Recycling programs
for this product may
not exist in your area.

ISBN-13: 978-0-373-73290-6

THE NANNY'S SECRET

Copyright © 2014 by Elizabeth Lane

Printed In U.S.A.

Books by Elizabeth Lane

Harlequin Desire

In His Brother's Place #2208
The Santana Heir #2241
The Nanny's Secret #2277

Harlequin Special Edition

Wild Wings, Wild Heart #936

Silhouette Romance

Hometown Wedding #1194
The Tycoon and the Townie #1250

Harlequin Historical

Wind River #28
Birds of Passage #92
Moonfire #150
MacKenna's Promise #216
Lydia #302
Apache Fire #436
Shawnee Bride #492
Bride on the Run #546
My Lord Savage #569
Navajo Sunrise #608
Christmas Gold #627
   "Jubal's Gift"
Wyoming Widow #657
Wyoming Wildcat #676
Wyoming Woman #728
Her Dearest Enemy #754
Wyoming Wildfire #792
Stay for Christmas #819
   "Angels in the Snow"

The Stranger #856
On the Wings of Love #881
The Borrowed Bride #920
His Substitute Bride #939
Cowboy Christmas #963
   "The Homecoming"
The Horseman's Bride #983
The Widowed Bride #1031
The Lawman's Vow #1079
Weddings Under a Western Sky #1091
   "The Hand-Me-Down Bride"
The Ballad of Emma O'Toole #1151

Other titles by this author
available in ebook format.

ELIZABETH LANE

has lived and traveled in many parts of the world, including Europe, Latin America and the Far East, but her heart remains in the American West, where she was born and raised. Her idea of heaven is hiking a mountain trail on a clear autumn day. She also enjoys music, animals and dancing. You can learn more about Elizabeth by visiting her website, www.elizabethlaneauthor.com.

For Tiffany

One

Dutchman's Creek, Colorado

HELP WANTED
Live-in nanny for newborn. Wolf Ridge area. Mature.
Discreet. Experience preferred.
Start immediately. Email résumé and references to
wr@dcsentinel.com

Wyatt Richardson glared at the stack of résumés on the borrowed desk. So far he'd interviewed three teenagers, a Guatemalan woman who barely spoke English, a harried mom with her own two-year-old and a grandmotherly type who confessed she got heart palpitations at high altitudes. His need for a qualified nanny bordered on desperation. But so far not one of the applicants was right for the job.

At least none of them had seemed to recognize him in his faded baseball cap. But that didn't solve his problem.

Maybe he should have gone through an agency instead of placing that blind ad through *The Dutchman's Creek*

Sentinel. But agencies asked questions, and this was a personal matter, demanding privacy. Not even his staff at the resort knew that his sixteen-year-old daughter, Chloe, had shown up on his doorstep almost nine months pregnant—or that she'd just given birth to a baby boy at the local hospital.

With a weary sigh he scanned the final résumé. Leigh Foster, 26. At least her age was in the ballpark he'd wanted to see. But the journalism degree from the University of Colorado wouldn't be much help. And her experience handling children was limited to some babysitting in high school. Glancing down the page he noticed she'd edited a defunct travel magazine and was currently working part-time for the local paper. He'd bet she was scrambling for money. Why else would an educated woman apply for this job?

Never mind. Just get it over with. He buzzed the receptionist, a signal to send in the next applicant.

High heels clicked down the tiled hallway, their cadence brisk and confident. An instant later the door of the small interview room opened. Wyatt's gaze took her in at a glance—willowy figure, simple navy blue suit, dark chestnut hair worn in a sleek pageboy. An Anne Hathaway type. He liked what he saw—liked it a lot. Unfortunately he was looking for a nanny, not a date.

"Mr. Richardson." Her long legs flashed as she strode toward the desk, hand extended. Her use of his name put Wyatt on instant alert. She worked for the *Sentinel* and would have known who placed the ad, he reminded himself. But the woman was a journalist. Did she really need a job or was she scoping out some juicy gossip for a story?

Either way, his first priority had to be protecting Chloe.

Rising, he accepted her proffered handshake. Her fingers felt the way she looked—slim and strong but surprisingly warm. Her tailored jacket had fallen open to reveal a coppery silk blouse. The fabric clung to her figure enticingly.

Yanking his gaze back to her face, Wyatt nodded toward the straight-backed chair opposite the desk. She settled onto the edge, one shapely knee crossed over the other in her narrow little skirt.

Sitting again, he perused her résumé, giving him a reason to take his eyes off her. "Tell me, Miss Foster. You appear well qualified for work in your own field. Why would you want a job as a nanny?"

Her lush mouth twitched in a sardonic smile. "I may be qualified, but times are tough. Right now I'm working twenty hours a week and camping out in my mother's guest room. She sells real estate, so she's struggling, too—and she has my younger brother to support. I'd like to contribute instead of feeling like a burden."

"So it's all about money."

"No!" She stared down at her hands. When she looked up again he noticed her eyes for the first time. Framed by thick, black lashes, they were the color of aged whiskey with intriguing flecks of gold.

"There are many factors involved. Most of my friends have children." The words sounded rehearsed. "I've been thinking that down the road a few years from now, if I don't get married, I might try adoption, or even have a child by a donor. Meanwhile, I'd love the experience of caring for a little baby. Of course I can't promise to stay for a long time…." Her husky voice trailed into a breath. "If you're still interested, could you tell me more about the job? Otherwise, I'll just leave now."

She clasped her hands on her knees, looking so vulnerable that Wyatt almost melted. He was interested all right—interested in getting to know this woman better. But he couldn't do or say anything that might make her hesitate to take the job. He needed a nanny for Chloe's baby, and right now Leigh Foster was his only option.

On the other hand, he had to make sure she wasn't out to exploit the situation.

Clearing his throat, he reached for the briefcase he'd left under the desk. "I'll need to run a background check, of course," he said, lifting out a manila folder. "But before we pursue this any further, would you be willing to sign a confidentiality agreement?"

Her eyes widened. "Of course. But why—?"

"You're a journalist." He slid a single page across the desktop. "And even if you weren't I'd demand your signature on this document. Protecting the privacy of my family is incredibly important to me. You must agree that whether you take the job or not, nothing you see or hear will be carried away—starting right now. You're not to publish it or share gossip with anyone, not even your own mother. Do I make myself clear?"

She leaned forward to scan the page—a boilerplate document outlining the legal consequences of sharing information in any form. The open neck of her blouse gave him a tantalizing glimpse of creamy flesh and black lace before he tore his eyes away. If he wanted her to take the job, it wouldn't do to be caught ogling her cleavage or any other delicious part of her. Especially since she'd be sharing his home.

"Any questions?" he asked her.

She straightened, impaling him with her stunning eyes. "Just one, Mr. Richardson. Could you spare me a pen?"

Leigh scrawled her name along the blank line at the bottom of the page. Maybe if she did it fast enough, he wouldn't notice that her hand was shaking.

The confidentiality agreement was no problem. Even without that piece of paper there was no way she'd reveal what she hoped to learn. But that didn't ease her nervous jitters. If Wyatt Richardson knew why she was really here, she'd be up to her ears in you-know-what.

The truth was she knew a lot more about the man than she was letting on. Even under that silly baseball cap she'd have recognized the local celebrity who'd put Dutchman's Creek on the map. In his younger days he'd been a daredevil downhill skier, winning several Olympic medals and enough product endorsements to make him rich. Coming home to Colorado he'd bought Wolf Ridge, a run-down resort that was little more than a hangout for local ski bums. Over the past fifteen years he'd built the place into an international ski destination that rivaled Aspen and Vail in everything but size.

That much was public knowledge. Discovering the details of his private life had taken some digging. But what Leigh learned had confirmed that she needed to be here today. There was no guarantee she'd be hired for the nanny job. But either way, she had to take this masquerade as far as it would go.

Right now, everything depended on her playing her cards carefully.

"Satisfied?" She slid the signed contract back across the desk. "I'm not looking for a story. I'm looking for a job."

"Fine. Let's see how it goes after we've talked." He slid the baseball cap off his head and raked a hand through his thick, gray-flecked hair. He'd be a little past forty, she calculated. His athlete's body, clad in jeans and a gray sweatshirt, was taut and muscular, his strongly featured face scoured by sun and wind. His eyes were a deep, startling Nordic blue. The year he'd won Olympic gold, a popular

magazine had named him as one of the world's ten sexiest men. From the looks of him, he hadn't lost that edge.

It was public record that he'd been divorced for more
than a decade. He looked as virile as a bull and, along
with that, was certainly rich enough to have women falling at his feet, but he'd managed to keep his sex life out of
the public eye—though, of course, in a small community
like Dutchman's Creek there was always talk. Not that it
mattered. She wasn't here to become one more notch on
Wyatt Richardson's bedpost.

Although the notion did trigger a pleasant sort of tingle
between her thighs.

"Tell me about the baby," she said.

"Yes. The baby." He exhaled slowly, as if he were about
to wade into battle. "My daughter's. She's sixteen."

"You have a daughter?" Leigh feigned surprise.

"Her mother and I divorced when she was young. I
didn't see much of her growing up, but for reasons I won't
go into now, Chloe and the baby will be staying with me."

"What about the father?" Her pulse shot to a gallop, the
pressure hammering against her eardrums. She willed her
expression to remain calm and pleasant.

"Chloe won't give me a name. She says he's history. I
take it he's just some boy she met while she and her mother
were living here. But if I ever get my hands on the little
bastard..."

One powerful fist crumpled the baseball cap. He released it with a muffled sound that could have been a
sigh or a growl.

"That's the least of my worries now. Chloe insists she
wants to keep her baby. But she doesn't know the first
thing about being a mother. Lord, she's barely more than
a baby herself." His cerulean eyes drilled into Leigh's.

"The nanny who accepts this job will be taking care of *two* children—the baby and his mother. Do you understand?"

Leigh had begun to breathe again. "I believe I do, Mr. Richardson."

"Fine. And please call me Wyatt." He rose, catching up the briefcase and jamming the cap back onto his head. "Let's go."

"Go where?" She scrambled to her feet as he strode around the desk.

"I'm taking you to the hospital to meet Chloe. If she thinks you'll do, I'll be willing to hire you for two weeks' probation. That should give me time to find someone else if things don't work out. We can discuss salary on the way back here."

Two weeks. High heels teetering, she struggled to keep pace with his strides. Next to a long-term job it was the best she could hope for. And even if he didn't hire her she'd at least get to see the baby.

"My vehicle's around back." He paused to hold the door for her. The October sun was blinding after the dim hallway of the small office building. Beyond the town, the mountain slopes were a riot of green-gold aspen, scarlet maple and dark stands of pine. The light breeze carried a whisper of winter to come—the winter that would bring snow to the mountains and skiers flocking to the high canyon runs.

"Careful." His hand steadied her elbow, guiding her around a broken piece of the asphalt parking lot. She could feel the power in his easy grip—a grip that remained even after they'd passed the danger spot.

She'd half hoped he'd be driving a sports car. But the only vehicle in the back parking lot was an elephant-sized black Hummer with oversized snow tires. "Sorry about the behemoth," he muttered. "This is my snow vehicle. My regular car's getting a brake job."

When he opened the passenger door for her, Leigh realized that the floor was thigh-high. There was no step, just a grip handle on the frame inside the door. There was no way she could climb up without making a spectacle of herself in the pencil skirt and high heels she'd worn to look professional for the interview. Maybe she should've worn jeans and hiking boots.

He stood behind her, saying nothing. For heaven's sake, was the man waiting for her to hitch up her skirt and give him a show?

Glancing back, she shot him an annoyed look. "If you wouldn't mind…"

His chuckle caught her off guard. "I was waiting for you to ask. If I were to just grab you, I'd be liable to end up getting slapped."

With that, he scooped her up in his arms as if she weighed nothing. Her breath stopped as his strong hands lifted her high and lowered her onto the leather seat. The subtle heat of his grip lingered as she fastened her safety belt. Her pulse was racing. As he strode around the vehicle and swung into the driver's seat, she willed herself to take deep breaths. Wyatt Richardson was a compellingly attractive man, capable of making her hormones surge with a glance from those unearthly blue eyes. But Leigh knew better than to go down that road. Let him get close enough to discover the truth about her, and she'd be up the proverbial creek.

And she wouldn't be the only one in trouble.

As the engine purred to life, she settled back into the seat. "So your daughter's in the hospital. When did she have the baby?"

"Yesterday morning. An easy birth, or so I was told.

She and the baby are doing fine. They should be ready to leave sometime tomorrow."

"What about the girl's mother? Is she in town to be with her daughter and see her grandchild?"

He winced as if she'd stuck him with something sharp. "Her mother's in Chicago with her new husband. Evidently the marriage is on shaky ground. That's why she chartered a plane for Chloe last week and sent her to me."

"I'm sorry, but that's monstrous."

"Don't judge her too harshly. The situation has us all thrown. I didn't even know Chloe was pregnant till the girl climbed out of a taxi and rang my front doorbell. Frankly, I'm still in shock."

And what about your poor daughter? Leigh thought it but she didn't say it. For now, at least, she'd be wise to tread lightly.

He turned onto the side road that led to the county hospital. "I didn't mean to dump all this on you before you met the girl. But at least you'll know what you could be getting into. Chloe's been through a devil of a time. And aside from taking her in and hiring somebody for the baby, I don't know how to help her through this."

"It sounds as if you care, at least. That should count for something."

A bitter laugh rumbled in his throat. "Say that to Chloe. She'll tell you that my caring's come about fifteen years too late."

He swung the Hummer into the parking lot and pulled into an empty space. After walking around to open the door on Leigh's side, he held up his arms. Taking her cue from him, she placed her hands on his muscled shoulders. His grip around her waist was brief as he lowered her to the ground. But as he released her, their eyes met. His were sunk into weary shadows—the eyes of a man who'd spent some sleepless nights. A worried man, unsure, perhaps, for the first time in his life.

For the space of a breath his big hand lingered on her hip. As if suddenly aware, he pulled it away and took her arm. "Let's go inside," he said.

Leigh was familiar with the hospital, a sprawling one-story maze of wings and hallways. Having visited several friends there, she knew her way to the maternity ward. "Were you here when the baby was born?" she asked as Wyatt walked beside her.

"I was wrapping up a meeting and missed the delivery, but I saw Chloe in recovery. They'd given her an epidural for the birth. She was still groggy when I left. She probably won't even remember I was there."

Leigh glanced down a side hall where the nursery windows were located. She was hoping to see the baby for a moment, but Wyatt kept walking on down the corridor, checking the room numbers. He paused outside a door that was slightly ajar. "I guess this is it."

"Go on in," Leigh said. "I'll wait out here until you're ready to introduce me."

Murmuring his thanks, he squared his shoulders, knocked lightly on the door and stepped into the room.

Chloe was sitting up in bed, peering into a small, round mirror as she dabbed mascara onto her eyelashes. With her mop of auburn curls, she looked like a little girl playing with her mom's makeup. How could this child be a mother?

"Hello, sweetheart," he said.

"Hello, *Daddy*." Her voice was edgy. The bouquet of pink roses he'd sent earlier had been shoved into a space above the sink.

Wyatt cleared his throat. "I'm told you have a beautiful little boy. How are you feeling?"

"How do you think?" She twisted the top onto the mascara tube. "I texted my friends. They're coming by to see the baby. His name's Michael, by the way. Mikey for now."

"Did you call your mother?"

She shrugged. "I sent a text. She's on her way to New York with *Andre*. He has some kind of gallery show."

"So she's not coming to see the baby?"

"Why should she? Mom's still in denial about being a grandma. Anyway, who needs her?" Chloe fished a lipstick out of her purse and swiped the burgundy hue onto her cupid's bow mouth.

Wyatt lowered himself onto a handy chair. "We need to talk, Chloe."

"What's to talk about?" She looked at him warily, as if bracing herself for a fight. "You already know I'm going to keep him."

Yes, she'd made that completely clear, despite his many arguments against it. But he wouldn't rehash that now, not when he could see how tired she looked. "I understand. And I hope you know that you and Mikey will have a home with me for as long as you need it. But what about the rest? Have you ever taken care of a baby?"

Her sky-blue eyes cast him a blank look.

"For starters…" He wrestled with the delicate question that needed to be asked. "How are you going to feed him?"

Her eyes widened. "You mean, am I…? OMG, no way! I'm not going around with saggy boobs for the rest of my life—and I do plan to have a life, Daddy. I want my baby, but you can't expect me to sit home with him all the time. As soon as you buy me a car, I'm going to—"

"The car can wait." It was all Wyatt could do to keep from snapping at her. "Meanwhile you've got a child to take care of. Do you even know how to change a diaper?"

She stared at him as if he'd just climbed out of a flying saucer.

"Goodness, Daddy. What do you think we're getting a nanny for?"

Waiting outside the half-opened door, Leigh heard everything. Wyatt had given her an inkling of what to expect. Now the impact of what she'd be dealing with smacked her full in the face. She could see what he'd meant when he'd said she'd have two children in her care. And Chloe sounded like a handful. Only the thought of the baby kept her from turning around and walking out of the hospital.

Seconds later he reappeared in the doorway, his face a mask of frustration. "Sorry you had to hear that," he muttered.

"It's just as well that I did." Following his lead, she allowed him to usher into the room. Chloe was sitting up against the pillows. Even in the drab hospital gown she looked like a petite little doll with Shirley Temple curls and china-blue eyes—almost as blue as her father's.

"Chloe," Wyatt said, "this is Miss Foster. Unless you have some objection, I plan on asking her to become your son's nanny."

The girl scrutinized her carefully. Leigh wondered what she was looking for. Chloe seemed to be wondering the same thing as uncertainty passed over her face. She stole a glance at her father, but he seemed to be replying to a message on his phone. "Fine," the girl said, clearly trying too hard to sound authoritative. "She'll do."

"Thank you." The less said, the better, Leigh resolved.

Chloe glanced toward the door, where the nurse had appeared with a blue-wrapped bundle. "I hope you're not staying much longer," she said. "My friends are coming over to see Mikey, and they'll be here any minute."

"We were just about to leave." Wyatt eased toward the door as the nurse entered.

"Wait!" Leigh said, seizing the moment. "Since I'll be helping with your baby, Chloe, would you mind if I held him for a minute?"

"Whatever."

Leigh felt her heart drop as the nurse placed the warm bundle in her arms. He felt so tiny, almost weightless. Scarcely daring to breathe, she pulled down the edge of the blanket to reveal the small, rosebud face. Little Mikey was beautiful, with his mother's blue eyes and russet curls. But it was his other features she looked for and found—the aquiline nose and square chin, the ears that didn't quite lie flat, the dark, straight brows—all coming together in one perfect package.

Leigh fought back welling tears. There could be no more doubt. She was holding her brother's child.

Two

With her emotions on the brink of spilling over, Leigh turned toward Wyatt. "Time for you two to get acquainted," she said, thrusting the blue bundle toward him.

He seemed to hesitate. Then his big hands took the slight weight, holding the child away from his body like a jar of live honeybees. His expression was a stoic mask. Leigh stifled her dismay. Wyatt hadn't asked for this little boy to come into his life, she reminded herself. Still it wouldn't hurt for him to show some affection. How could anyone with a soul not love a baby?

Leigh noticed that Chloe was focused on the sight of her son in her father's arms as well, but Chloe's expression was difficult to read. Sadness? Wistfulness? Worry? Envy? Dismay? Maybe all of the above—or maybe none of them. Whatever she was feeling, she didn't say a word. Leigh sighed, the task before her looming like a mountain. It wouldn't be easy, maybe not even possible. But in the time allowed, she would do her best to help these people become a family.

* * *

Wyatt gazed down at the tiny face. The eyes that looked up at him were blue like Chloe's, but with an openly trusting quality to them that Chloe's hadn't held in years. He saw his daughter in the wispy amber curls and full, heart-shaped mouth. But some features were unfamiliar. The unknown boy, who'd taken what he wanted without a second thought, had left traces of himself, too.

The boy who'd derailed Chloe's young life.

If Wyatt had known about the pregnancy early on, would he have discouraged her from having this baby? Chloe was his only child, and he'd had such plans for her—college, maybe a career and a good marriage with children born at the right time. But it was too late for questions and regrets. The baby was here and she seemed determined to keep it. They would have to make the best of a bad situation.

But Lord, where would he find the wisdom? Where would he find the patience to be there for his daughter and grandchild? It just wasn't in him.

Sensing his tension, perhaps, the baby broke into a plaintive wail. The knot in Wyatt's stomach jerked tight. Now what? He didn't know anything about babies, especially how to deal with crying ones.

"You take him." He shoved the mewling child into Leigh's arms. Out of the corner of his eye, he saw Chloe flinch. Something here didn't seem right. But whatever it was, Wyatt didn't know how to fix it. As a man, he'd taken pride in his ability to handle any situation. But right now he felt just plain lost.

Leigh cradled the baby close. He stopped crying and snuggled into her warmth, his rosebud mouth searching instinctively for something to suck. Aching, Leigh brushed a fingertip over the satiny head. He was so tiny, so sweet and so helpless. How could she do this job without losing her heart?

From the open doorway, delighted teenage squeals shattered the stillness.

"Chloe! Is that your baby?"

"OMG, he's so little!"

"Let me hold him!"

Three pretty, stylish girls swarmed into the room, laden with wrapped gifts and shopping bags, which they piled on the foot of the bed. With a sigh of relief, Leigh surrendered little Mikey to one of them. Her eyes met Wyatt's across the crowded room. He nodded toward the door. It was time for the grown-ups to leave.

"You look rattled. How about some coffee?" Wyatt's hand brushed the small of Leigh's back, setting off a shimmer of awareness as he guided her into the corridor.

"Thanks, that sounds good. I'd guess we're both rattled." Leigh's knees were quivering. Only the arrival of Chloe's girlfriends had saved her crumbling composure.

Kevin's baby. Her own little nephew. And she couldn't risk telling a soul.

Leigh and her teenage brother had always been close. Last spring Kevin had confided to her that he'd gotten a girl pregnant. *Chloe Richardson—her dad owns Wolf Ridge and she goes to that snooty private school. She texted me that she was pregnant. I offered to...you know, man up and be responsible. But she said to forget it because she planned to get rid of the kid. She was moving away and never wanted to hear from me again. Promise me you won't tell Mom, Leigh. It would kill her.*

Leigh had kept her promise, believing the issue would never surface again. Then a few days ago, as she was proofing the ads for the paper, she'd discovered that Wyatt

Richardson needed a nanny. Some simple math and a discreet call to the hospital had confirmed all she needed to know.

Telling Kevin was out of the question. After a long phase of teenage rebellion he was finally thinking of college and working toward a scholarship. The news that he had a son could fling the impulsive boy off course again. Worse, it could send him blundering into the path of a man angry and powerful enough to destroy his future. Leigh couldn't risk letting that happen. But she wanted—needed—to know and help Kevin's baby.

"Here we are." Wyatt opened the door to the hospital cafeteria. "Nothing fancy, but I can vouch for the coffee." Finding an empty table, he pulled out a chair for Leigh. She waited while he went through the line and returned with two steaming mugs along with napkins, spoons, cream and sugar.

Seating himself across from her, he leaned back in his chair and regarded her with narrowed eyes. "Well, what do you think?" he demanded.

Leigh took her time, adding cream to her coffee and stirring it with a spoon. "The baby's beautiful. But I get the impression your daughter is scared to death. She's going to need a lot of help."

"Are you prepared to give her that help?"

Leigh studied him over the rim of her mug. She saw a successful man, a winner in every way that mattered to the world. She saw a tired man, his jaw unshaven and his eyes laced with fatigue. She saw a father at his wits' end, and she knew what he wanted to hear. But if she couldn't be honest in everything, she would at least be honest in this.

"Assuming the job's mine, I'll do my best to give her some support. But make no mistake, Wyatt, it's the baby I'll be there for. Chloe's *your* child. If you think you can step aside and leave her parenting to me, we'll both end up failing her. Do I make myself clear?"

For an instant he looked as if she'd doused him with a fire hose. Then a spark of annoyance flared in his deep blue eyes. One dark eyebrow shifted upward. Had she said too much and blown her chance? As he straightened in his chair, Leigh braced herself for a storm. But he only exhaled, like a steam locomotive braking to a halt.

"Good. You're not afraid to speak your mind. With Chloe, that trait will come in handy."

"But did you *hear* what I said?"

"Heard and duly noted. We'll see how things go." He whipped a pen out of his pocket and wrote something on a napkin. "This is the weekly salary I propose to pay you. I trust it's enough."

He slid the napkin toward her. Leigh gasped. The amount was more than twice what she'd anticipated. "That's very…generous," she mumbled.

"I expect you'll earn every cent. Until Chloe and the baby settle into a routine, you'll be needed pretty much 24/7. After things calm down we'll talk about schedules and time off. In the next few days, I'll have a formal contract drawn up for you. That nondisclosure document you signed will be part of it. Agreed?"

"Agreed." Leigh felt as if she'd just consigned away her soul. But it was all for Kevin's baby. She took a lingering sip of her coffee, which had cooled. "So when do you want me to start?"

"How about now? The nursery needs to be set up. I'd intended for that to happen before the baby was born, but Chloe couldn't make up her mind on what she wanted. It can't wait any longer—you'll just have to decide for her. Earlier today I called Baby Mart and opened an account. After I take you back to your car, you can go there and pick out whatever the baby's going to need—clothes, diapers, formula, a crib, the works. Everything top-of-the-line. I've arranged for special delivery by the end of the day." He rose from his chair, all energy and impatience. "After that, you should have a couple of hours to resign from the paper, pack your things and report to my house."

"You want me there *tonight?*"

"If the baby's coming home tomorrow, we've got to have the nursery ready and waiting. Will you need directions to the house?"

"No. I know where you live." No one who'd been to Wolf Ridge could miss the majestic glass-and-timber house that sat like a baron's castle on a rocky bluff, overlooking the resort. Finding her way shouldn't be a problem, even in the dark. But Leigh couldn't ignore a feeling of unease, as if she were being swept into a maelstrom.

Wyatt Richardson was a man who'd started poor and achieved all he had through force of will. Mere moments after she'd agreed to work for him, he was taking over her life, barking orders as if he owned her—which to his way of thinking, he probably did.

Since he was her employer, she would put up with a certain amount of it. But if the man expected her to be a doormat he was in for a surprise. She would be little Mikey's advocate, speaking up for his welfare, even if it meant bashing heads with Wyatt.

Kevin's child had been born into a family with an immature teenage mother, an uncaring grandmother and a reluctant grandfather, whose idea of family duty was to turn everything over to the hired help. In the hospital room, when she'd given Wyatt the baby, he'd handled the tiny blue bundle like a ticking bomb. He seemed to be in denial about his grandson's very existence, never referring to him by name, only calling him "the baby."

Changing things would be up to her. She could only hope she was wise enough, and tough enough, for the challenge.

Wyatt boosted Leigh into the Hummer, struggling against the awareness of his hands sliding over her warm curves. Her fragrance was clean and subtle, teasing his senses to the point of arousal. Her long legs, clad in silky hose, flashed past his eyes as she climbed onto the seat. What would she do if she knew he was imagining those legs wrapping his hips?

She'd probably kick him halfway across the parking lot.

What had gotten into him? Didn't he have enough trouble on his hands with Chloe and the baby? Did he really need to complicate things with an attraction toward the woman he'd hired to be the nanny?

He'd never had trouble getting bed partners. All he needed to do was stroll through the resort lodge and make eye contact with an attractive female. If she was available, the rest would be easy.

So why was he suddenly craving a woman who came with a hands-off sign?

Maybe that was the problem. With Chloe and the baby sharing his house, an affair with the nanny would be a dicey proposition. For that matter, with Chloe in residence, bringing any woman to his bedroom would be a bad idea— just one of the ways his life was about to change.

But right now, that was the least of his worries.

Closing the door, he walked around the vehicle and climbed into the driver's seat. Leigh had fastened her safety belt and was attempting to tug her little skirt over her lovely knees. Wyatt willed himself to avert his eyes.

"Just for the record," he said, starting the engine, "we

don't hold with formal dress at the house. Pack things you'll be comfortable in, like jeans and sneakers."

Or maybe you should dress like a nun, to remind me to keep my hands off you.

"Jeans and sneakers will be fine." Her laugh sounded strained. "I don't suppose your grandson will care what I'm wearing."

"My grandson. Lord, don't remind me. I'm still getting used to that idea."

"This isn't about you. It's about an innocent baby who'll need a world of love—and a young girl learning to be a mother. You'll need to be there for both of them."

Isn't that where you come in? Wyatt knew better than to voice that thought. Leigh had expressed some strong notions about family responsibility. But wasn't he doing enough, taking Chloe and her baby under his roof, buying everything they needed and hiring a nanny to help out?

Back when he was married, Tina had complained that he was never home—but blast it, he'd been busy working to support his wife and daughter. He'd been determined to give them a better life than he'd had growing up.

Even after the divorce he'd taken good care of them. He'd given Tina a million-dollar house, paid generous alimony and child support and always remembered Chloe's birthday and Christmas with expensive gifts—gifts he'd never have been able to afford if he hadn't poured so much time and energy into the resort.

Hadn't he done enough? Was it fair that he was expected to finish raising a spoiled teenager with a baby so Tina could run off with her twenty-seven-year-old husband?

"There's my car." Leigh pointed to a rusting station wagon parked outside the office he'd used for the interviews. One look was enough to tell him that the car would never make it up the canyon on winter roads. He would need to get her something safe to drive before the first snowfall.

Wyatt pulled the Hummer into a nearby parking place. Steeling himself against her nearness, he climbed out and opened the door on the passenger side. Leigh was waiting for him to boost her to the ground. She leaned outward, her hands stretching toward his shoulders. Wyatt was reaching for her waist when her high heel caught on the edge of the floor mat. Yanked off balance, she tumbled forward on top of him.

He managed to break her fall—barely. For a frantic instant she clung to him, her arms clasping his neck, her skirt hiked high enough for one leg to hook his waist. But his grip wasn't secure enough to hold her in place. Pulled by her own weight, she slid down his body. Wyatt stifled a groan as his sex responded to the delicious pressure of her curves pressed against him so intimately.

Her sudden gasp told him she'd felt his response. He glimpsed wide eyes and flaming cheeks as she slipped downward. Then her feet touched the ground and she stumbled back, breaking contact. They stood facing each other, both of them half-breathless. Her hair was mussed and one of her shoes was missing. She tugged her skirt down over her thighs.

"Sorry," she muttered. "I didn't hurt you, did I?"

Wyatt tried his best to laugh it off. "No, I'm fine. But that maneuver could've gotten us both arrested."

Her narrowing gaze told him she didn't appreciate his humor. It appeared that, despite her naughty little skirt, Miss Leigh Foster was a prim and proper lady. All to the good. He'd be wise to keep that in mind.

"Excuse me, but I need my shoe." She teetered on one high-heeled pump. Wyatt retrieved the mate from the floor of the SUV, along with her brown leather purse. She took them from him, wiggling her foot into the shoe.

"You'll be all right?" he asked her.

"Fine. I'll be going straight to Baby Mart from here, then home. I should be knocking on your door by nightfall."

"Plan on dinner at the house, with me. And remember you're to say nothing about Chloe and her baby. All the people at Baby Mart need to know is who's paying for the order and where it's to be delivered." He fished a business card out of his wallet and scribbled his private cell number on the back. "Any questions or problems, give me a call."

"Got it." She tucked the card in her purse, pulled out her keys and walked away without a backward glance. He watched her go, her deliberate strides punctuating the sway of her hips. Her clicking heels tapped out a subtle code of annoyance. Could she be upset with him?

Wyatt watched the station wagon shudder to a start, spitting gravel as it pulled into the street. No, he hadn't read her wrong. The woman was in a snit about something.

Maybe she thought he'd pushed her too hard, giving her orders right out of the starting gate. But since he was paying her salary, it made sense to let her know what he expected. After all, he was her employer, not her lover.

And that, he mused, was too damned bad.

Returning to his vehicle, he pulled into traffic and headed toward the road that would take him out of town. He'd gone less than two blocks when he saw something ahead that hadn't been there earlier. City workers were digging up the asphalt to fix what looked like a broken water main. Neon orange barricades blocked the roadway. A flashing detour sign pointed drivers to the right, down a narrow side street.

He'd made the right turn and was following a blue Pontiac toward the next intersection before he realized where he was. A vague nausea congealed in the pit of his stomach. He never drove this street if he could help it. There were too many memories here—most of them bad.

Most of those memories centered around the house partway down the block, on the left. With its peeling paint and weed-choked yard, it looked much the same as when he'd lived there growing up. Wyatt willed himself to look away as he passed it, but he'd seen enough to trigger a memory—one of the worst.

He'd been twelve at the time, coming home one summer night after his first real job—sweeping up at the corner grocery. The owner, Mr. Papanikolas, had paid him two dollars and given him some expired milk and a loaf of bread to take home to his mother. It wasn't much, but every little bit helped.

His mouth had gone dry when he'd spotted his father's old Ranchero parked at the curb. Pops had come by, most likely wanting money for the cheap whiskey he drank. He didn't spend much time at home, but he knew when his wife got paid at the motel. If she gave him the cash, there'd be nothing to live on for the next two weeks.

Wyatt was tempted to stay outside, especially when he heard his father's cursing voice. But he couldn't leave his mother alone. Pops would be less apt to hurt her if he was there to see.

Leaving the bread and milk by the porch, he mounted the creaking steps and pushed open the door. By the light of the single bulb he saw his mother cowering on the ragged sofa. Her thin face was splotched with red, her eye swollen with a fresh bruise. His father, a hulking man in a dirty undershirt, loomed over her, his hands clenched into fists.

"Give me the money, bitch!" he snarled. "Give it to me now or you won't walk out of this house!"

"Don't hurt her!" Wyatt sprang between them, pulling the two rumpled bills out of his pocket. "Here, I've got money! Take it and go!"

"Out of my way, brat!" Cuffing Wyatt aside, he raised a fist to punch his wife again. Wyatt seized a light wooden chair. Swinging it with all his twelve-year-old strength, he struck his father on the side of the head.

The blow couldn't have done much damage. But it hurt enough to turn the man's rage in a new direction. One kick from a heavy boot sent the boy sprawling. The last thing Wyatt remembered was the blistering whack of a belt on his body, and his mother's screams....

Forcing the images from his mind, Wyatt turned left at the intersection and followed the detour signs back to the main road. His father had taken the money that night. And while his mother rubbed salve on his welts, he'd vowed to her that he would change their lives. One day he'd be rich enough to buy her all the things she didn't have now. And she would never have to change another bed or scrub another toilet again.

He'd accomplished his goals and more. But his mother hadn't lived to see his Olympic triumph or the successes that followed. She'd died of cancer while he was still in high school.

His father had gone to prison for killing a man in a bar fight. Years later, still behind bars, he'd dropped dead from a heart attack.

Wyatt had not attended the burial service.

He'd put that whole life behind him—had made himself into a new man who was nothing at all like his dad.

So why did he feel so lost when it came to dealing with his daughter?

Not that he didn't love Chloe. He'd never denied the girl anything that might make her happy. He'd been the best provider a man could be and not once—not ever—had he raised a hand against her. But now it slammed home that in spite of all the work he'd done and the things he'd bought, he still didn't know the first thing about being a father.

Three

Turning onto the unmarked side road, Leigh switched her headlights on high beam. Until now, she hadn't been worried about finding Wyatt's house. But the moonless night was pitch-black, the thick-growing pines a solid wall that shut off the view on both sides.

She hadn't planned on arriving so late. But everything back in town had taken longer than she'd expected. When the clerk at Baby Mart had helped her make a list of furniture and supplies, Leigh had been staggered at how much it took to keep one little baby in comfort—and how long it took to choose each item. By the time she'd left the store her head was pounding, her feet throbbing in her high-heeled pumps.

She'd stopped at the paper to tell her boss she was quitting, then headed home. Kevin and her mother had hovered around her bed as she threw clothes and toiletries into her suitcase. They'd demanded to know what was going on. Leigh had mumbled something about a secret assignment, assuring them that she'd be fine, she'd keep in touch, and they could always reach her on her cell phone. They probably suspected she'd gone to work for the CIA, or maybe that she was running from the Mafia.

She hated keeping secrets from her family. But there was no other way to make this work. Kevin's baby son needed her help; whatever it took, she would be there for little Mikey.

A large, pale shape bounded into her headlights. Her foot slammed the brake. The station wagon squealed to a stop, just missing the deer that zigzagged across the road and vanished into the trees.

Shaken, she sagged over the steering wheel. What was she doing, driving up a dark mountain road to move in with a man she barely knew—a man who made her pulse race every time his riveting indigo eyes looked her way?

The memory of that afternoon's encounter, when she'd tumbled out of the SUV and into his arms, was still simmering. The clumsy accident must have been no more than a simple embarrassment for Wyatt. But the brief intimate contact had flamed through *her* like fire through spilled gasoline. Wyatt Richardson was a good fifteen years her senior. But never mind that—the man exuded an aura that charged the air around him like summer lightning. How was she going to keep her mind on work if her pulse ratcheted up every time he came within ten feet of her?

Right now Wyatt should be the least of her worries. Tucked into her purse was the one item she'd bought with her own cash at Baby Mart—a thick paperback on infant care. Truth be told, her experience with babies consisted of a few bottles and diaper changes. What she didn't know about umbilical cords, fontanels, bathing and burping would fill…a book.

Once the nursery was set up, she planned to spend the rest of the night reading. She'd always been a quick study.

This time she would have to be. She couldn't fake it with a baby—it was become an expert before tomorrow or risk doing something wrong and possibly harming the child.

Braking for the deer had killed the engine and left her badly spooked. Starting the car again, she drove at a cautious pace up the winding road. An eternity seemed to pass before the trees parted and she found herself looking up a rocky slope. From its top, light shone through towering windows.

Minutes later she pulled up in front of the house. She stepped out of the car to see Wyatt standing on the broad stone porch, his arms folded across his chest.

"What kept you? I was about to send out a search party. Why didn't you call?" He sounded like the parent of a teen who'd missed curfew.

"Sorry. My phone died. And everything took longer than I'd expected. I didn't even take time to change." She glanced down at her rumpled suit, then down further to where her feet had swollen to the shape of her pumps. Opening the back of the station wagon, she reached for her suitcase, but Wyatt was there ahead of her. He snatched up the heavy bag and carried it into the front hall.

"Did the order from Baby Mart get here?" she asked.

"It arrived a couple of hours ago. I had the delivery man put the crib together, but everything else is still in boxes. You'll have your work cut out for you."

"There's no one here to help?" She'd expected to see a servant or two but there wasn't another soul in sight.

His eyebrow quirked upward. "Just you—and me. Dinner's warming in the oven if you're hungry."

"I'm starved." And she was, even though she hadn't given food a thought until now. "Don't tell me you cook," she said.

"Lord, no. I keep snacks and breakfast food in the

kitchen, but when I want a real meal, I have it delivered from the restaurant at the lodge. Tonight it's lasagna." He lowered the suitcase to the floor. "You can leave your things here till we've eaten."

He ushered her into the great room, its cathedral roof shored by massive, rough-hewn beams. The north wall, overlooking the resort, was floor-to-ceiling glass. No blinds were needed. Seeing inside from below would be next to impossible.

The logs in the huge stone fireplace had burned down to coals, leaving the space pleasantly warm. After kicking her shoes off her swollen feet, Leigh slipped off her jacket, tossed it back over her suitcase and followed Wyatt. Off to her right she glimpsed a formal dining area, but it appeared they'd be eating in the brightly lit kitchen, where the steel-topped table had been set for two.

Wyatt seated her and used a padded glove to lift the foil-wrapped pan out of the oven. There was a fresh salad on the table, along with a baguette, a bottle of vintage claret and two glasses.

"I'll pour and you dish." He handed her a spatula. "It might be overcooked."

"My fault for being late. Sorry." Leigh scooped two squares of lasagna onto the plates. It didn't look over-cooked, and it smelled heavenly.

"Eat hearty. We've got plenty work ahead of us, getting that nursery set up."

"You said *we*. Does that mean you're planning to help?"

"With the heavy lifting, at least. But you'll be the one organizing things. I hope you plan to change into something more comfortable."

"Of course." Leigh's face warmed as his cobalt eyes lingered on her. The silk blouse she'd worn with the suit had always been a little snug. She'd forgotten that problem when she'd taken off her jacket. She scrambled to change the subject. "I still find it hard to believe you don't have help in this big house—in addition to me, of course."

"You mean like a butler and a chauffeur and a cook?" His eyes twinkled, an unexpected surprise. "You've been watching too many episodes of *Masterpiece Theatre*. A gaggle of servants hanging around would drive me crazy. I can load the dishwasher, answer my own doorbell and drive my own car. And I have a cleaning crew up from the lodge every Wednesday to keep the place looking ship-shape. Believe me, I like my peace and quiet."

She took a sip of wine and speared a sliced mushroom from her salad. It would be a waste of words, reminding him now, but Wyatt's precious peace and quiet was about to be shattered.

Leigh's room was on the second floor. Like the rest of the house, its decor was rustic and masculine with an eye to comfort. The queen-sized bed featured a decadent European-style featherbed and duvet. A hand-woven Tibetan rug covered much of the hardwood floor. Wooden shutters masked the tall windows.

One wall was decorated with framed black-and-white photos of the Himalayas. Among them was an image of a grinning, bearded Wyatt between two Sherpa porters. As Leigh stripped off her blouse, skirt and pantyhose, it was as if his mocking eyes watched her every move.

She would have to do something about that picture.

A side door opened into the nursery, which was piled with bags and boxes from Baby Mart. Zipping her jeans and tugging her sweatshirt over her head, she prepared to do battle with the mess. It was going to be a long night. And her tortured feet would feel every step she took.

Wyatt had just unpacked a solid oak rocker and was

situating a cushion on the seat. He glanced up as she padded barefoot into the nursery.

"That's more like it," he said, taking in her outfit. "But where are your shoes?"

Leigh wiggled her swollen toes. "Too many hours in stilettos. I'm so footsore I can't even wear my sneakers."

"That's no good." He rose, gesturing toward the chair. "Maybe I can help. Sit down."

She hesitated. "We really need to get started here."

"Sit. That's an order."

Leigh sank onto the padded seat. Being bossed rankled her, but she was on his clock, and if he could do something for her feet, who was she to argue?

Dropping to a crouch, he cradled her left foot between his hands. "Trust me. I've dealt with enough sports injuries to pick up a few tricks."

His strong hands began kneading her foot, fingers pressing the arch as his thumbs massaged the bones and tendons between her toes. Leigh could feel herself relaxing as the pain eased. Delicious sensations trickled up her leg. She closed her eyes. A moan escaped her lips.

He chuckled. "Feels good, does it?"

"Mmm-hmm. You could do this for a living." Her mind began to wander forbidden paths, imagining how those skilled hands would feel in other places. She hadn't been in a physical relationship since breaking her engagement, eleven months ago. Now she felt her body awakening to Wyatt's masculine touch. And she couldn't help remembering that they were alone here, with a bed in the next room....

But what was she thinking? Sleeping with Wyatt was a crazy idea. Any intimacy between them would just make it that much harder for her to hold on to her secrets.

With a mental slap, Leigh shocked herself back to reality. When she opened her eyes, Wyatt was looking up at her as if he'd detected something in her face. Her cheeks warmed. Had he guessed what she'd been thinking?

"How's your room?" He broke the awkward silence. "Will it be all right?"

"It's lovely—although I may not be able to roll myself out of that bed in the morning."

"Chloe chose that room for you. She wanted you next to the nursery, where you could hear the baby at night."

"And where will Chloe be?"

"Her room's downstairs. She says she doesn't want his crying to wake her up."

So, what's wrong with this picture? Leigh bit back an acerbic comment. She'd known she was getting into a prickly situation. That was why she'd taken the job in the first place. But this was no time to climb on her soapbox— especially since the issue would need to be addressed with Chloe, not the girl's father.

"I can guess what you're thinking." He switched to her other foot, skilled fingers kneading away the soreness. "But for now I want you to cut the girl some slack—give her time to get back on her feet, physically and emotionally. When her mother had to choose between her husband and her pregnant daughter, Chloe found herself on her way to the airport with her bags. As if she hadn't been through enough already, dealing with the pregnancy on her own." Wyatt's fingers pressed harder against Leigh's arch, almost hurting. "So help me, if I ever find the irresponsible jerk who took advantage of a young girl's trust and then just walked away…."

"I think we'd better get to work." Leigh pulled free and scrambled to her feet, uncertain she could trust herself not to rise to her brother's defense if Wyatt continued in that vein. It wasn't as if Kevin hadn't offered to stand by

Chloe. As for what had happened—Kevin had told her it had been after a party, with both of them more than a little drunk. No trust—or even love—involved. No one taking advantage. Just two reckless kids being stupid.

But the result of their thoughtless act was the little miracle she'd held for the first time today.

Not that she could explain any of that to Wyatt. Not now, and probably not ever.

Reaching for a box of linens, she began unwrapping crib pads, sheets and towels. "These will all need to be washed and dried before we use them," she said. "There's baby soap here somewhere. If you'll point me toward the laundry room, I'll get started."

"It's just off the kitchen—you'll see it when you go downstairs. Meanwhile, I'll unpack more of these boxes and recycle the cardboard. You can put everything away when you get back here."

"Thanks." Leigh found the pink soap box, bundled up the linens and headed for the stairs. She needed a break from Wyatt's overpowering presence, and the laundry gave her an excuse. His drive had won Olympic glory and built one of the finest ski resorts in the state. But up close and personal, his magnetism could be an emotional drain. Her physical attraction to him only complicated things.

It would be easier after tomorrow, with the baby here. She'd have something to focus on, something to love— *no, not to love.* She was here to give Kevin's son a good start in life. Sooner or later she would have to let go and walk away. If she allowed herself to fall in love with little Mikey, the final break would rip her heart out.

Wyatt stood alone on the second floor balcony. He'd expected to be worn out after helping Leigh set up the nursery. But they'd finished a couple of hours ago, and he was still too restless to sleep.

Leigh had been a whirlwind of efficiency—all business. There'd been no more sign of the chemistry that had flared between them when he'd rubbed her feet. But he hadn't forgotten it. He'd always maintained that the sexiest thing about a woman was her face. The sight of Leigh's face, her eyes closed, her lips parted in a blissful moan, had jolted his imagination into overdrive. He'd pictured that lovely dark-framed face on a pillow, her entranced expression deepening as he pleasured her....

Wyatt took a moment to enjoy the memory, then closed the door on it. For now, at least, a foot massage was as intimate as he planned to get with Miss Leigh Foster. Bed partners were a dime a dozen. But he'd already learned that a suitable nanny was worth more than gold.

A sliver of moon had risen above the canyon. Far below, beyond the trees, the lights of the resort spread like a jeweled carpet. The summer concert season was over, but the autumn color drew hikers to the slopes and sightseers flocking to the hotels, shops and restaurants. And the cold season was coming soon. Already his crews were inspecting every inch of the runs and lifts, getting ready for the first big snowstorm.

A light breeze, smelling of winter, cooled his face. He always savored this time of year and the changes it brought. But the changes happening now were like nothing in his experience.

Leigh was right. Chloe was going to need him. But how could he even begin to nurture her, discipline her and give her the support she needed? From his own father, Wyatt had inherited a legacy of neglect and abuse. What if the traits that made a good parent were simply missing in him? It was that fear that had made him keep his distance when she was a baby, herself. He'd missed the chance to get to know her, to build the kind of relationship that would help him understand how to be there for her. Could he trust himself to build that relationship now? Where did he even begin?

As for the baby… He couldn't begin to wrap his brain around that reality. Not tonight. But if he wasn't sure how to be a father after all these years, then he couldn't believe that Chloe was prepared to be a mother when she was barely more than a child herself. Having a child could destroy her future. Since she'd arrived, he'd tried over and over again to help her realize that the best thing for all of them would be to give the little boy up to a good family. The message hadn't gotten through, but perhaps things would change now that the baby was here. Once she realized that having a baby wasn't like having a new doll, the girl might come to her senses.

Meanwhile, there was Leigh. He was depending on her to maintain a level of sanity he could live with. So far, she'd proved as efficient, hardworking and practical as she was pretty. He could only hope she had the skill to care for the baby and the patience to deal with the red-haired hellion that was Chloe at her worst.

The weariness he'd been holding back too long crashed in on him. Time he got some rest. It was late, and tomorrow he'd be bringing Chloe and the baby home from the hospital. The day was bound to be trying.

Stepping back inside, he headed toward the stairs. That was when he glanced down the dark hallway and noticed the sliver of light under the closed door of Leigh's bedroom. Discretion told him to ignore it. But it was one-thirty in the morning. What if something was wrong? What if she was sick or in some kind of trouble?

Outside the door he paused to listen. Hearing nothing, he rapped lightly on the rough-hewn wood. When there was no answer, he pressed the latch and inched the door open.

Lamplight glowed on Leigh in bed, propped against two oversized pillows. She was dead asleep, her eyes closed, her head drooping to one side. The thin strap of her silky black nightgown had slipped off one shoulder to reveal the upper curve of a satiny breast.

Had she been waiting up for *him?* But that notion wasn't worth the time it took to kick it to the curb. Nothing in tonight's behavior could've been read as an invitation.

So why hadn't she just turned off the light and rolled over? In the next instant he found the answer. On the duvet, where it could have fallen from her hand, lay a thick paperback book. Drawing closer, Wyatt could make out the title—*Baby Care for the New Mother.*

Leigh had fallen asleep cramming for her job.

So her claim to be experienced in childcare was something of a stretch. A smile teased the corners of Wyatt's mouth. He wasn't ready to fire Leigh. But he wanted to let her know, in a subtle way, that he was wise to her little fib.

Tired as she was, she'd probably sleep until morning. If she woke to find the book on the nightstand and the lamp switched off that should be enough to give her a clue.

Leaving his shoes in the hallway, he stole across the carpet to the bed. Close up, her lush beauty was even more tempting—ripe lips softly parted, lashes like velvet fringe against her satiny cheeks, and a fragrance that stirred his senses like a seductive night breeze.

As he leaned over her to pick up the book, she shifted against the pillow. The black ribbon strap slipped lower on her shoulder, giving him a glimpse of one rosebud nipple peeking above the lace trimming the neckline.

His sex rose like a flagpole, straining against his jeans. Wyatt cursed silently as his fingers closed around the open book. They were alone in the house. If Leigh opened her eyes, what would he do? Would he mumble an excuse and leave like a gentleman, or would he be true to his manly nature?

Silly question. But never mind. Leigh had shown him her proper side. Nothing she'd said or done had indicated that she'd take kindly to being awakened with a man bending over her bed.

Giving in to his better judgment, Wyatt laid the book on the nightstand, switched off the lamp and, with a last regretful glance, left the room.

Four

Leigh opened one eye, found the bedside clock and groaned. Seven-thirty. Of all mornings to oversleep, she had to pick this one.

When she swung her legs off the bed, she noticed something on the nightstand. The baby book. How many chapters had she gotten through before she fell asleep? And how many of those pages could she actually remember? She could only hope she'd have time for a refresher while Wyatt was picking up Chloe and the baby.

She was walking away from the bed when it struck her—she had no memory of closing the book and laying it on the nightstand. And she certainly hadn't switched off the bedside lamp before dropping off. Somebody had looked in on her in the night. And that somebody was wise to her lack of experience.

She stifled a groan. Not a great way to start a new job.

The aroma of fresh coffee wafted under the door and into her nostrils. Her shower would have to wait. Right now she needed to get herself downstairs and convince Wyatt she had everything under control.

Yanking on her jeans and a black turtleneck, she splashed her face, brushed her teeth and ran a hasty comb through her hair. For now, that would have to do.

Still barefoot, she followed her nose, padding down the stairs and into the kitchen. Wyatt sat sipping coffee at the table, dressed in jeans and a dark blue cashmere sweater that matched his eyes. Those eyes took her measure, from her bare toes to her still-tousled locks. "Coffee's on the counter," he said pleasantly. "I put out a mug for you. How did you sleep?"

"Too well. That featherbed is decadent."

"And your feet? You're going to need your shoes today."

"They'll be fine." Leigh inhaled the fragrant steam as she poured the coffee. "Cream?"

"In the fridge. If there's anything you'd like for the kitchen, you can order it through the lodge by phone or email. The number and email address are on the contact list by the phone. It'll usually be delivered by the end of the day."

"Thanks. I'll make a list after I find out what Chloe would like. How soon will you be picking her and the baby up?"

"They should be ready any time after ten. But I changed my mind about going. I'm sending you instead."

"Me?" A reflexive grab barely saved Leigh's mug from crashing to the floor.

"Since I've already paid the hospital there's no reason for me to be there. And I've got an important phone conference scheduled for ten o'clock." He pulled a chair out from the table. "Sit down, Leigh. We need to talk."

She sat, perching on the edge of the chair like a child about to be punished. What now?

He turned his seat to face her. "When I hire someone I usually give them a written job description. I've never hired a nanny before, but we both need to know what's expected."

Leigh nodded, holding her tongue. Better to keep still than to speak and make a fool of herself.

"You've made it clear that your first priority will be the baby. That's fine. But you need to be aware of my other concerns."

"Of course." She willed herself to meet his gaze. His eyes were the color of a deep mountain lake—and at this moment, just as cold, she thought.

"One concern, a big one, is my family's privacy. Chloe's friends know about the baby, of course. So does the hospital staff. All of them have been warned to keep the matter under wraps. I won't have my daughter falling prey to gossip, especially if the press gets involved. And I won't have her future reputation tainted by one careless mistake."

How could anyone look at that beautiful boy and call him a mistake? Keeping that thought to herself, Leigh nodded her understanding.

"Is that why you want me to drive her home—so she and the baby won't be seen with you and recognized?"

"In part." He rose to put his empty cup in the sink. "That will be one of your prime responsibilities—keeping a lid on things. For now, at least, Chloe's not to take the baby out in public—for safety reasons as well as privacy. You're to track her online activity, Twitter, Facebook, anything that could be seen by the wrong people—"

"No."

He stared in surprise as she rose. "No?"

"I'm a nanny, not a spy. I understand your wanting to protect her, Wyatt, but the one who monitors her computer and phone should be her father."

His scowl darkened. She plunged ahead before he could interrupt.

"Think about it. I'm here in a nurturing role, to care for the baby and help Chloe learn to be a mother. She needs to trust me. If that's to happen I can't wear two hats. I can't support her and police her at the same time."

"So you're saying I should be the bad guy."

"If that's what you want. You must have surveillance people at the resort. You'll find a way."

He took his time rinsing his mug and stowing it in the dishwasher. "All right, you win—for now. But there's one more thing."

"I'm listening." Leigh remained on her feet, as did he.

"Chloe's young and she's bright. If she could put this incident behind her, she could still have a promising future."

Incident? A baby?

"If she sticks with her choice to raise the boy, I'll respect her decision," he continued. "But you and I both know it will change her life, and not for the better. What I'm hoping is that soon she'll be sensible and give him up for adoption—to a good family, of course. I trust you'll do your best to steer her in that direction. In the long run it would be better for her and for the baby. Don't you agree?"

Leigh stood rooted to the floor as his words sank in. *Sensible? Yes. But oh, so cold.* She found her voice.

"You're Chloe's father, and I can see where you're coming from. I'll give the matter some thought."

"Then let me give you something else to think about. I'm sure you're aware that if Chloe gives up the baby it will mean the end of your job here. In the spirit of fairness, if that becomes her decision and you support her in it, I'm willing to offer you a severance package of twenty-five thousand dollars. I'll have it written into your contract."

Leigh willed herself to appear calm. Inside, she was

reeling—not so much because of the amount, but because of his icy determination, and his assumption that her help could be bought.

"That's a generous offer," she replied. "I'll keep it in mind. But right now it's getting late. If I'm to be at the hospital by ten, I need to get ready...."

With her voice threatening to break, she turned and headed out of the kitchen.

"Leigh, one more thing."

She froze but didn't turn around.

"I just thought you should know. You have your shirt on inside out."

Stifling a groan, she fled up the stairs.

Wyatt stood on the balcony, watching the black sport wagon disappear behind the trees. He'd had the vehicle brought up from the resort for Leigh's temporary use. The Hummer would be hard for Chloe to climb into, and the girl would turn up her pretty nose at that rust bucket Leigh had driven here.

Later today he'd contact his supplier for a sturdy wagon with all-wheel drive. Chloe would be pestering him for a sports car but she wasn't getting it before spring, and only then if she showed some responsibility. For now, she and Leigh could share the new vehicle.

Wyatt could afford as many luxury cars as he wanted; but the mountain property didn't have enough level ground to waste on a big garage. The one at the rear of his house had room for just three vehicles—the Hummer, the new SUV he planned to buy and the Bentley that was his one indulgence, a vintage 1976 Corniche that he'd restored himself after his divorce. He'd be getting it back from the mechanic later today with new brakes. He also owned a couple of snowmobiles, which he kept in a shed, mostly for emergencies.

A scrub jay fluttered onto a nearby pine branch, cocked its head and regarded him with curious eyes. The bird's presence reminded Wyatt why he'd chosen to live in this remote spot overlooking the canyon. The place was wild and clean, and he'd done his best to keep it that way with solar panels on the roof and state-of-the-art recycling technology. For the past ten years he'd enjoyed his privacy here. Now all that was about to change.

Maybe it wouldn't be all bad. He'd enjoyed seeing Leigh come into the kitchen this morning, fresh-faced, rumpled and hastily dressed, as if she'd just tumbled out of bed. The warm, pleasant feeling had lingered like an aura—until they'd started talking.

Leigh had barely spoken while he helped secure the baby carrier in the car's backseat; and she'd driven off without even saying goodbye. Her silence had spoken volumes about his offer and what she thought of it.

Wyatt didn't take well to being denied. In fact, if he'd known how headstrong Leigh was, he might not have hired her in the first place.

Not just headstrong, he mused. There was something unsettling about the woman. Something that didn't add up. She was too sophisticated, too self-assured to settle for a job like this one. So why had she taken it? Her reasons from the interview didn't hold water. If she was as experienced with babies as she'd implied, why had she been reading that baby book in the middle of the night?

Who was she? What did she really want?

Leigh managed to hold herself together until she was sure the car couldn't be seen from the house. Then she pulled off the road, pressed her shaking hands to her face and allowed reality to sink in.

Wyatt Richardson didn't want his precious grandson. And he expected *her* to talk Chloe into giving the boy up. He'd even offered her money.

How was she supposed to deal with that?

She knew that Wyatt was thinking of Chloe's future. As far as he was concerned, the baby was an unlucky accident to be hushed up and sent away for the good of all concerned. Her heart rebelled at the thought of it...but she forced herself to take a deep breath and think with her head.

Was he right? Would little Mikey be better off with two adoptive parents than with an unmarried teenage mother and a grandfather who only wanted him gone? Maybe. But even if Chloe decided to take the adoption route today, Leigh was certain it would still take time to find the right parents and get through the paperwork. And in the meantime, the baby was going to need someone on *his* side, to fight for his rights and his welfare. For now, she would be that someone. And she would do everything in her power to see that whatever choice was made would be driven by love, not by expediency.

But she couldn't be there forever. When the time came, and she'd done all she could...

Unable to finish the thought she started the car and pulled back onto the road.

She arrived at the hospital thirty minutes later to find Chloe sitting on the bed, wearing sweats, flip-flops and an impatient pout. "Where's Daddy?" she demanded.

"Home waiting for you." Leigh fixed her face in a determined smile. "You're all checked out. As soon as the nurse gets here with Mikey we'll be on our way."

As if on cue, the nurse appeared with the baby, tightly

wrapped in a new white blanket. Chloe brightened. "Put him down. I want to see him in his new outfit!"

With her son on the bed, she unwrapped the blanket to reveal what looked like a puppy costume—a white stretch jumpsuit with brown spots and a matching hat that sported droopy brown ears. "Isn't that precious?" she cooed. "My BFF Monique gave him that. Got to send pictures." Fishing her cell phone out of her purse, she leaned over the baby and began snapping photos.

Leigh took advantage of the delay to feast her gaze on her nephew. Even since yesterday he'd changed. His cheeks were rounder, his features more defined. Delicate golden lashes fringed his eyelids, framing dark blue eyes, like his grandfather's. Baby expressions flickered across his face— a frown, a look of wide-eyed wonder, and then something that could almost have been a smile. Even in that silly dog costume, his beauty took Leigh's breath away.

While Chloe was busy texting, Leigh folded back the cuffs that covered his hands. They were oversized like Kevin's, the digits long and thin. When she brushed his palm, his baby fist closed around her finger. She felt the strong clasp all the way to her heart.

"Away we go!" The nurse, who'd left the room, returned with a wheelchair. Still texting, Chloe took her seat, leaving Leigh to wrap the baby and grab the take-home bag the hospital had provided.

With a no-nonsense manner, the nurse picked up the baby and thrust him at Chloe. "Put away that phone, dearie, and take your little boy," she snapped. Chloe did as she was told, though she stuck out her tongue when the nurse turned away. Watching, Leigh took a mental note. She had a lot to learn about the girl.

Minutes later they were on their way, with Mikey in the backseat, buckled into his carrier. Chloe had chosen to sit in front with Leigh. She took her phone out of her purse and checked her messages.

"Can we stop for a Coke?" she asked.

Leigh kept her eyes on the road. "Your father wanted me to bring you straight back. There'll be sodas in the fridge."

Chloe fell into a pouting silence, playing with her phone and finally putting it back in her purse. "What did Daddy say your name was?" she demanded.

"It's Leigh Foster. You can call me Leigh."

"Leigh Foster." There was a long pause before she asked, "Are you by any chance related to a jerk named Kevin Foster?"

Leigh's pulse lurched. She took a few breaths to collect herself before she answered. "There are a lot of Fosters in Dutchman's Creek. We take up half a page in the phone book."

The answer seemed to satisfy the girl—for now. But she was far from finished. "So what made you want to be a nanny? Why would anybody want a job changing poopy diapers?"

Leigh feigned a shrug. "I needed the work. The pay is good. What's more, I happen to like little babies, diapers and all."

"And my rich, handsome, single daddy had nothing to do with it?"

"Nothing at all." Like the rest of Leigh's answers, that was—technically—true.

"Plenty of women have tried to land him, even a couple of movie stars who came here. You'd recognize them if I told you who they were. They were pretty in person. A lot prettier than you."

Wyatt's daughter was testing her, Leigh realized. She was probing for weak spots that could be exploited later to get what she wanted. It wasn't going to work.

"How are you feeling, Chloe?" she asked, changing the subject. "Still pretty sore, I imagine."

"Are you kidding? I hurt all over! Especially my boobs! The nurse said my milk was coming in. Gross! Don't they have some pills I can take for that?"

"They used to. Then they found out the pills increased the chance of breast cancer. So you'll just have to tough it out till the swelling goes away—unless, of course, you decide to nurse your baby. It's not too late."

"No way! That would be so gross!"

"Then I'll see about getting you some ice packs at the house." Leigh swung the car onto the private road. "But don't expect to jump right back into your life. It'll take you a few weeks to get back to normal."

Chloe winced as a tire jounced over a fallen rock. "How come you know so much? Have *you* ever had a baby? You certainly look old enough."

"I'm twenty-six. And the answer is no, I haven't had a baby. But most of my friends have children. I've talked with them about what it's like."

If only she could talk to them now. But even if she didn't name names, confiding in her friends that she was taking care of a baby would be skating the edge of the agreement she'd signed. If Wyatt Richardson had the means to monitor his daughter's emails and phone calls, he could, and likely would, do the same with hers.

"Ever been married?" Chloe asked.

"Never."

"Ever lived with a guy?"

"In Denver, for about a year. We were engaged." Leigh didn't like talking about her past, but if it would help her build rapport with the girl, she was willing to open up a little.

"And you didn't get married? What happened?"

"The usual." Leigh managed a wry laugh. "He cheated on me."

"Guys can be such douche bags." Chloe sounded more like a world-weary forty-year-old than a girl barely out of middle school.

"What about your father?" The question popped out before Leigh could think the better of it.

"Daddy is who he is. He likes his privacy and his women. And he likes being in control. He's pretty generous. He'll give you anything you ask for—except his time. Anything else you want to know, ask the people he works with—they see more of him than I ever did. I can't say he'd win many prizes as a father. But at least he doesn't pretend to be somebody he isn't."

Leigh hesitated, weighing her response.

"I wouldn't get involved with him if I were you," Chloe said. "He doesn't let anybody get too close, even when he is around. That's part of why my mother left him, I think. Maybe—"

The jangle of her cell phone cut off whatever she'd been about to say. "Hi, Daddy...Yes, we're on the mountain road...Mikey's in the back. He's fine. We're all fine... See you in a few minutes." She ended the call with a sigh. "Such a control freak! I swear he checks on every breath I take!"

Leigh held her tongue and kept on driving. The task ahead of her loomed like Pike's Peak. Could she do enough to mend this dysfunctional family for Mikey's sake—and still keep her heart intact?

She'd never been much of a churchgoer. But as they rounded the last steep curve, her lips moved in a silent prayer for wisdom.

Five

Wyatt came outside as the car pulled up to the porch. After opening the door on Chloe's side, he reached in to help her stand. With a muttered "I'm not an invalid," she waved him away and climbed out by herself. For a young woman who'd just given birth she looked all right. But imagining what she'd been through was like a kick in the gut—or a bad dream.

Lord, she was a mother now—his little girl, who wasn't much more than a child herself.

Leigh had opened the back door and lifted the baby carrier off its base. "Mikey must've liked the car ride," she said, beaming down at Chloe's son. "He's fast asleep. Just look at him, Wyatt. Isn't he beautiful?" Moving deftly, she blocked Wyatt's path to the house, and thrust the baby carrier into his line of vision.

Wyatt sensed what the woman was up to. He'd made no secret of his feelings toward the baby or his hope that Chloe would give the child up, and it was clear that Leigh disapproved. He wanted to ignore her question, and the baby she was holding out toward him. The last thing he wanted was to become attached to the little mite. But there was no mistaking the steel in Leigh's eyes and the set of her jaw. She wouldn't step aside until he'd taken a good look at his grandson.

Tilting the carrier toward him, she folded back the blanket to reveal a miniature face as perfect as a flower. Wyatt's throat went dry. Yesterday, holding the baby, he'd been focused on his own discomfort and his anger toward the unknown father. Now he saw an innocence that threatened to wrap around his heart and crush it like a root tendril crushing a stone.

Whatever he was feeling, it hurt. And it wasn't what he wanted to feel.

"Well, what do you think of him?" Leigh asked.

"He's a handsome boy, all right." The words came with effort. "But I can't say much for the dog outfit. A gift from one of Chloe's friends, I take it."

At the sound of his voice, the baby yawned adorably and opened calm, curious eyes. His cheek dimpled as he smiled—not a real smile, of course. Not yet. But it was a good imitation.

Something tightened in Wyatt's chest. He sensed the closing of a trap.

"I'm starved!" Chloe called from the doorway. "What's to eat around here?"

"Pizza's in the oven." He was grateful for the diversion. "Double cheese supreme, your favorite. Are you up to eating in the kitchen or can we bring a tray to your room?"

"Kitchen." She sounded cranky, probably hurting. "After that I'm going to sleep. That hospital bed sucked, and the food sucked even worse."

At least she seemed glad to be home. Wyatt held the door so Leigh could carry the baby inside. "The pizza's for you, too, Leigh. In fact, you're welcome to share the table at all our meals. We're family here, for whatever that's worth."

Her smile was like the sun coming out. "Thanks. As the hired help, I was wondering about that."

"You shouldn't. Like I said, you've been watching too many episodes of *Masterpiece Theatre*."

"Then I hope you won't mind my wanting to cook now and then. You have a great kitchen. It's a shame to waste it."

"Knock yourself out." He followed his daughter into the kitchen where the table was already set for three. Chloe didn't even glance his way as she pulled the pizza pan out of the oven. Things were bound to be prickly with Chloe for a while. He could only hope having Leigh as a buffer would ease the tension.

Chloe took her seat, scooped two pizza slices onto her plate and popped the tab on a can of diet soda. Leigh placed the baby carrier on the far end of the table before she sat down. The baby was awake and doing his best to suck on his fist.

"Shouldn't you put him to bed?" Chloe asked.

"Mikey's part of your family now," Leigh said. "As long as he's not fussing, it's good for him to be here, listening to friendly voices."

"Whatever." Chloe shrugged and went on eating. "You're the expert."

Wyatt cast her a frown as he took his seat. In open defiance of his wishes, Leigh was doing all she could to bond the baby into the family. What he couldn't understand, given the offer he'd made her, was *why*.

He found himself watching the little fellow. Darned if that fist wasn't a real challenge. When he couldn't get it into his mouth, he became visibly frustrated. But he kept on trying—at least he wasn't a quitter. His hands flailed at his face until—*ouch*—he hit himself in the eye.

The blow must've hurt, or at least surprised him. He flinched sharply and began to cry—not a mewling whimper, but a full-blown howl. What a pair of lungs.

Leigh was out of her chair like a shot, scooping him up and gathering him against her shoulder. Rocking him gently, she made little soothing sounds until his cries faded to baby hiccups.

Chloe watched with anxious eyes. "Is he all right, Leigh?"

"He's fine. But he might be hungry. The hospital gave us a few bottles of prepared formula. Keep an eye on him. I'll go get one."

She lowered Mikey into the carrier, but she'd no sooner let him go than he started to bawl again. Chloe stared at her son with a pained look. "Why is he yelling like that? Isn't there something you can do to stop it?"

"Sorry, but I'm afraid you'll have to get used to it. We all will." Leigh picked up the infant and thrust him toward the girl. "He likes to be held. Give it a try. I'll be right back."

Wyatt didn't miss the panic that flashed across his daughter's face. Chloe was feeling overwhelmed—and he couldn't say he blamed her. "Give the boy to me," he heard himself saying. "I can hold him for a minute."

With a look of surprise, Leigh passed him the squirming bundle. Making a cradle with his arms, Wyatt gathered the little squalling creature against his chest. How could anything so small be so demanding? Young Mikey was already bossing the adults around as if he owned the place.

"Hello, Mikey." The words emerged as a growl from Wyatt's tight throat. Startled by the unfamiliar voice, the baby stopped crying and gazed up at him with those stunning eyes. Acting on instinct, Wyatt began to rock him gently, singing the first song that popped into his head—a timeworn ditty about the fate of a daredevil skier.

"He was headed down the slope doin' ninety miles an hour…"

He looked over to see that Chloe was watching with an enraptured expression on her face. "OMG, Daddy, look at him. He loves it. Did you ever sing that song to me?"

Wyatt replied with a shrug. As busy as he'd been when Chloe was small—and as nervous as he'd been about turning into his own father—he hadn't spent much time with her. Maybe if he had, they'd have a better relationship now. But it was too late to change the past. He could only hope to salvage her future—a future without a fatherless baby in it.

Leigh had found one of the bottles in the bag the hospital had provided. The formula was room temperature. That had to be all right. By tomorrow she'd have to be up to speed on how to prepare the bottles herself. So much to learn. How long could she keep faking it before she got herself in trouble?

Walking back to the kitchen, she paused in the doorway. Wyatt was cradling Mikey in his arms, his head bent over the baby. She could hear his rumbling song, and although she couldn't make out the words, she could tell that both he and his grandson were having a good time. Listening to his playful voice and watching the fall of sunlight on his hair, she felt something soften inside her. Maybe there was hope for this man—and this family—after all.

As she entered the room, Wyatt glanced up and stopped singing. "Take this little rascal," he said. "I wasn't cut out to be a nursemaid."

Reaching from the side, Leigh lifted the baby to her shoulder. "Want to try feeding him, Chloe?"

"You do it. I'm tired, and you're the expert."

Leigh took a seat at the far end of the table and settled Mikey in her arms. She hadn't bottle-fed an infant since her high school babysitting days, but how hard could it be?

Mikey had been fed in the hospital, so he knew the ropes. As soon as the nipple brushed his lips, he latched on and began chomping like a hungry piglet.

"Quite an appetite the boy's got." Wyatt was frowning but he couldn't disguise the note of pride in his voice. So far he was proving an easy conquest. Chloe, on the other hand, seemed to be going out of her way not to look at them. Maybe the girl just needed time.

Or maybe she was scared to death of being a mother.

Mikey had already downed half the small bottle. Was he drinking too much? Leigh slipped the nipple out of his mouth. The baby let out a howl of protest, keeping it up until she replaced it. "He seems to be strong-willed," she said. "Now, how do you suppose he came by that?"

She glanced from father to daughter. Chloe was eating and still refusing to look their way. Wyatt's only response was a deepening scowl. So much for her lame attempt at humor.

In the next few minutes Mikey finished off the formula and seemed satisfied. Now, if Leigh remembered right, he'd need to be burped to get rid of any air he might have swallowed. Raising him against her shoulder she began patting his back. Nothing. And now he'd started fussing. Was she doing something wrong?

She was about to change tactics when she heard a startling belch. She began pulling him back off her shoulder a little to see if he was all right when something warm and wet washed over the shoulder of her black turtleneck, soaking the ends of her hair and trickling down her chest and back.

"OMG!" Chloe was staring, goggle-eyed. Wyatt was struggling to keep a straight face. When Leigh lifted the baby fully away from her shoulder, she saw that the dog outfit was drenched in spit-up formula.

If Mikey was upset about the mess, he didn't show it. In fact his attention seemed to be focused on something else. As Leigh held him at arm's length, a bubbling sound rose from his diaper, along with an unmistakable aroma.

Wyatt cocked an eyebrow. "I think it's time for Mikey to be excused, Leigh. We'll save you some pizza."

Clutching her wet, smelly nephew, Leigh fled toward the stairs.

By the end of the day Leigh was worn out. She'd peeled off Mikey's reeking clothes, wiped, sponge bathed and changed him, fed him a small amount, burped him, this time with a protective cloth, and put him down for a blessed nap. While he was sleeping she'd put his soiled garments and hers to soak in cold water, tidied herself up, rigged a couple of makeshift ice packs for Chloe's swollen breasts, and sterilized the unused bottles and nipples she'd bought at Baby Mart.

She'd barely had time to wolf down two slices of warmed-over pizza before Mikey woke up again, fussing and wanting to be held. Babies learned fast how to get what they wanted.

With Chloe deep in exhausted slumber and Wyatt gone off in the car without saying where, the house was quiet. Snuggling the warm little body in her arms, she sank into the rocking chair. Mikey seemed to like the rocking motion. She could feel him relaxing against her. His eyes were calm and alert. If only her mother could see him. Once she got over the shock, she would fall in love with the little boy.

It was a shame that that could never happen, especially

since Leigh's mother had voiced her yearning for a grand-child many times. She'd been so happy about Leigh's engagement to Edward and so dejected over the breakup. Leigh had never told her the whole story—how she'd walked into the apartment to find Edward in bed with a coworker, and learned that he'd been cheating on her all along.

Would she ever trust a man again? But the answer to that question was on hold. Right now, and for the foreseeable future, the most important male in her life was the one in her arms.

The room darkened into twilight. Mikey had closed his eyes. His even breathing told her he'd fallen asleep. Carrying him as if he might break, Leigh tiptoed to the crib and eased him down on his back. He was as limp as a worn-out puppy, arms flung outward, hands curled into tiny fists.

With a last tender look, she picked up the receiver for the baby monitor, made sure it was working and slipped out of the room.

At the far end of the hallway was a cozy sitting area with a gas fireplace, well-stocked bookshelves and a state-of-the-art TV. It would be bliss, Leigh thought, to sink into the sofa and spend a mindless hour staring at whatever was on the screen. But right now she needed fresh air.

Double glass doors opened onto the upstairs balcony. Stepping outside, she set the monitor on a handy chair, leaned on the rail and inhaled the cool, piney fragrance of an October night. Far below, the lights of the resort glimmered in the dusk, climbing the ski runs and flowing down the bed of the canyon. This was Wyatt's kingdom, which he'd built over the years into a mecca of glamour.

Having done her homework, Leigh knew that Wyatt was vastly rich. The resort with its hotels and businesses, lodge, ski runs and surrounding properties, along with some major investments and holdings, had to be worth well over a billion dollars. But she'd seen firsthand how modestly he lived. Even this house—beautiful as it appeared—was built more for comfort than for display. It struck her that in placing it on this lonely bluff, overlooking the resort, Wyatt had set up his own private world—a world apart from the lavish milieu below. Did that private world have room in it for a pair of new additions?

She remembered how she'd seen him earlier today, singing to Mikey as he cradled the tiny boy in his arms. Behind the domineering, hard-driving facade he showed the world, the man had a tender side—a side she wouldn't mind seeing more of. Besides, there was something sexy about a man holding a little baby.

Even without the baby, Wyatt was one of the most compelling men she'd ever met. Last night, when he'd massaged her feet, she'd been close to panting. It wouldn't have taken much to push her past the limits of common sense. And if she didn't get herself under control, it wouldn't take much again....

A stray breeze, smelling faintly of wood smoke, cooled her damp hair. The night had turned chilly, but she wasn't ready to go inside. The stars were coming out, so many, so bright, undimmed by the lights of town. Far below, through the pines, she could make out the glow of headlights coming up the road. Her pulse quickened.

It had to be Wyatt.

Wyatt had picked up the Bentley at the resort, where the only mechanic he trusted had delivered it. He savored the feel of the vintage auto as he drove it up the mountain road, flying around the curves for the fun of it. With the first heavy snow, the car would be stored in the heated garage. Until then he could enjoy having it back in good repair.

As he drove, he kept a sharp eye out for deer. Leigh had mentioned almost hitting one last night. Her near miss was a reminder for him to be careful.

His thoughts circled back to Leigh—as they'd been circling all day. The woman puzzled, intrigued and frustrated him. She had the kind of classy sex appeal that made him want to fling her over his shoulder and haul her into his bed. But why would such a woman apply for a nanny job? What was she after?

Her background check had come back squeaky clean—not so much as a parking ticket. No bankruptcies. No pressing debts. Her education and work record exactly matched her résumé. She appeared to be smart and capable, and anyone with eyes could see how she felt about little Mikey.

But when it came to baby care, Leigh was obviously flying blind.

Catching her with that baby book had roused his suspicions. Today's incident had confirmed them. Anyone experienced with babies would have known Mikey might spit up. Hellfire, even *he* knew better than to burp an infant without putting a towel on his shoulder. But he'd seen the shock on Leigh's face. She'd been totally unprepared for the drenching she got.

Whatever else she might be, she definitely wasn't an experienced nanny. Not that he was planning to fire her. She was conscientious, hardworking and damned easy on the eyes. But he meant to discover Leigh's hidden agenda—by any means it took.

Earlier, he'd resolved not to lay a hand on his new employee. But getting up close and personal might be the only way to pry out her secret. A little pillow talk could accomplish wonders. Besides, it was bound to be fun.

Whistling under his breath, he rounded the last curve in the road and swung the Bentley toward the garage.

* * *

Leigh was still on the balcony when the car pulled up to the house. She heard the garage close, then the sound of Wyatt's footsteps crossing the porch. There was no reason to think he'd be coming upstairs. His bedroom, which she'd never seen, was on the main floor, flanked by his office and a private den. After today, he was likely ready for solitude.

The baby monitor was still silent, the night sky so glorious that she couldn't bring herself to go back inside. Standing at the rail, her eyes tracing the path of the Milky Way, she felt alone in the darkness. The last thing she expected was to feel a soft weight settle around her shoulders.

"Take my jacket," Wyatt's voice murmured in her ear. "Can't have you freezing out here."

"Thanks." She snuggled into his alpaca coat, her heart thundering as his arms wrapped it around her. "I haven't seen a sky like this in years. Too much light in town."

"I know. It's one of the reasons I built up here." His arms tightened, drawing her back against his chest. Against her better judgment she sank into his warm strength. His nearness was deliciously comforting.

"How's Chloe?" he asked. "I brought Chinese in case anybody's hungry."

"We can warm it up tomorrow. Chloe took a pain pill and went to bed. She was fast asleep when I last checked."

"And the baby?"

"He's asleep, too. But I have the monitor in case he wakes up."

A chuckle vibrated in his throat. "You've had quite the day yourself."

"I know. I took a few minutes to shower and change but I wouldn't be surprised if I still smell like baby spit."

He nuzzled her hair, taking his time. A thread of heat

uncurled in the secret depths of her body, shimmering upward. She felt her nipples pucker inside her bra. Oh, this wasn't smart. She should make her excuses and go inside. But her feet refused to move.

"Can't smell a thing. Just soft, clean, lovely hair." His lips brushed the tip of her ear. Her breath eased out in a long, whispered sigh. Common sense told her that Wyatt Richardson was up to something. But she'd been too long alone, too long angry and hurting, to pull away from the comfort he was offering.

And—Leigh forced herself to face the truth—she'd been thinking about this man all day. She'd wanted him from the moment she'd fallen out of his Hummer and into his arms.

Six

"I have a question for you, Leigh." His breath stirred her hair. His voice was bedroom husky; but something in his tone told her romance wasn't the upmost thing on his mind. "I'm hoping we can talk this over and come to an understanding."

Leigh had been careening toward the brink of surrender. But she gave herself a mental splash of cold water. "Go ahead."

"I've told you where I stand on Chloe's keeping her baby. But you've made it equally clear you don't agree."

She stiffened, her defenses prickling. A moment ago he'd seemed bent on seduction. Now she feared she was about to be fired. What kind of game was he playing?

"You have every right to feel as you do," he continued. "But what I don't understand is your motive—for shoving Mikey into the middle of the family and making sure Chloe and I interact with him. You must know that I don't *want* to get attached to the little mite. And I'm not sure I want Chloe to get too attached to him, either. That's why

I offered you a bonus to help her make a sensible decision. If it's more money you want—"

"You think this is about *money?*" She pulled away and spun to face him. "This is about Mikey! He's not some stray puppy you're trying to give away. He's a baby, Wyatt! He's Chloe's son and your grandson—your own flesh and blood. True, he might be better off with the right adoptive parents. But if Chloe makes that decision it should be because she *loves* him enough to want what's best for him instead of what's easiest for her. And the same goes for you! That innocent little boy deserves better than to have you turn your back on him!"

Wyatt stood frozen, looking as if she'd slapped him. Had she said too much? Was she about to get her walking papers?

"I see." His voice was expressionless. "That leaves me with another question. As a nanny, you've been winging it pretty well. But I'd bet my Bentley you're no more qualified for this job than I am. Why are you so passionate about a baby you didn't know existed until yesterday? What's your stake in all this?"

Dread congealed in the pit of Leigh's stomach. She'd revealed too much; and now Wyatt was within a sliver of stripping away her subterfuge.

Should she come clean and tell him everything, exposing her brother to Wyatt's fury and possible ruin?

Or should she risk a bluff—the only one that came to mind?

There was no way she was going to get Kevin in trouble and cause pain to her mother. The bluff was her only remaining choice.

"Leigh, I asked you a question." Wyatt's voice was as stern as his expression.

"Yes, I know…" With time running out, she had to act

fast. Flinging her arms around his neck, she pulled his head down and pressed her mouth to his in a desperate, devouring kiss.

Wyatt went rigid. A growl of surprise escaped his throat. Then his reflexes kicked in. Whatever game the woman was playing, he'd be only too happy to play along.

His arms caught her close, molding her curves against his solid body. A quiver went through her as he took control, his kiss utterly possessing her. Her lips parted, welcoming the playful thrust of his tongue. When his hands slid under her shirt, unclasping her bra in a single deft motion, she made no move to stop him. If this was an act, it was a good one, Wyatt told himself. He could feel the surging heat of her response. He knew his women, and this one showed every sign of wanting what he had to give.

His coat slipped off her shoulders to fall around their feet. She moaned as his hand moved over her bare back. His thumb skimmed the satiny edge of her breast, lingering just long enough for a tease. His mouth nibbled down her throat.

She was delicious, like hot buttered rum on a winter night.

Her chest arched against him in a clear invitation for more. Wyatt's fingers slid under one cup of her lacy bra to stroke her breast—small, but so firm, so perfect.... She gasped as he brushed her taut nipple, and then, as his palm cupped her, she made a little melting sound and pressed against him. His sex was hot and hard, threatening to rip out the rivets in his jeans. He knew she could feel it.

He kissed her again, taking time to savor those ripe, swollen lips. "So *this* is why you applied to work here?" he muttered half-teasingly.

"Mm-hmm...I've had a crush on you for years, and this

was my chance." She strained upward for another kiss with what appeared to be sincere eagerness. Not that he was fooled. She was probably lying through her pretty teeth about having planned this all along, but he believed she truly did want him at this moment and, besides, he was enjoying this too much to care. Sooner or later he'd get to the truth. Right now he had more urgent things on his mind.

Leigh was losing control. She'd meant to distract Wyatt from his line of questioning, maybe even convince him that she'd come here because of him. But the man had taken charge and was sweeping her along like a twig in an avalanche.

His lips nibbled hers with an easy restraint that made her ache for more. His hand rested on her bare breast, his thumb stroking her nipple to a throbbing, exquisitely sensitive nub. Heat streamed through her body, driven by her pounding heart. Where her hips pressed the solid ridge of his erection, the contact triggered spasms of need. She hadn't asked to want him like this, hadn't expected to. But the sensations that pounded through her body were too powerful to deny.

"You're so damnably sexy, Leigh." His free hand moved down the hollow of her back to dip below the waistband of her jeans. His fingers invading her panties, stroking the diamond shape at the base of her spine. "I've wanted you from the moment you walked into that interview in that hot little skirt of yours. Those legs…"

His touch was driving her to a frenzy. She whimpered and shifted her hips. Nuzzling her mouth again he let his hand glide around to rest on the flat of her belly. Somewhere in her brain, alarm sirens blared a warning. But Leigh was past hearing. His touch felt so good….

Breathless, she waited for his fingertips to glide lower.

Wetness soaked the crotch of her panties. She pressed against his hand, anticipating…

"We're in the wrong place for this," he muttered. "Come on." Keeping her in the circle of his arm, he propelled her back inside and down the hall toward her room.

"Chloe…the baby…" she whispered anxiously.

"They're asleep, and we can be quiet." He pulled her inside and closed the door. His mouth caught hers in a powerful kiss that sent whorls of heat pulsing through her body. His tongue probed hers, thrusting, caressing in an unmistakable pantomime of what he had in mind as he guided her toward the bed. His borrowed jacket, along with her shirt, bra, jeans and panties, left a trail across the floor.

Her arms wrapped his neck, fingers raking his hair as his kisses grazed her face, her throat, her breasts. The hollow between her hips had gone molten. Heaven help her, she wanted this man. She'd wanted him from the first instant their eyes locked.

"Tell me to leave, and I'll leave," he muttered in her ear. "But you'd better tell me now."

"Wyatt, I'm a big girl. And as the saying goes, this isn't my first rodeo. I know tonight isn't forever. I just want to enjoy it—and enjoy you. No strings attached."

One dark eyebrow quirked upward. "Well, now, that's refreshing. So we'll leave it at that—for the present, at least."

Leigh's hands found the hem of his cashmere sweater and underneath it, the chiseled contours of his athlete's body—the rippling back, the rock-solid abs, the tender, sensitive nipples that triggered a moan when she skimmed them with her fingertip.

With a murmur of impatience, he lowered her to the bed, then stripped off his clothes and added protection to his jutting arousal. There would be no tender words between them, no wooing, no promises, nothing between them but pure, pleasurable lust. And right now that was enough.

Climbing into the bed he caught her in his arms. Leigh could feel his length and bulk along her belly. She could almost imagine him inside her, filling the hungry, hidden place that had been empty too long. Her need deepened to an ache.

His hand readied her, stroking the moist, tender folds. As his finger slid into her, riding on her slickness, she came with a little gasping shudder.

"Yes…" she whispered. "Now. Please."

Laughing softly, he mounted between her eager legs and entered her with one long, gliding push. Her breath eased out in a sigh of bliss. The feel of him was pure heaven.

Neither of them was in the mood to take things slowly. As her legs wrapped him, their thrusts became a wild ride, fast and hard and joyous. She met each push with her hips, deepening the contact as her climax swirled and burst like a sky full of Independence Day fireworks.

He grunted, quivered and then relaxed against her. "Not bad for the first time," he chuckled.

With a gentle kiss he rolled off her, stood and padded into the bathroom, leaving Leigh curled blissfully in bed.

A wail arose from the crib in the adjoining room. Yanked back to reality, Leigh stumbled to her feet and flung on her robe. Mikey's plaintive cries tore at her heart.

Flinging open the door, she burst into the nursery. In the glow of the night-light, Mikey lay in the crib, fussing and waving his fists. As soon as Leigh picked him up and gathered him close, his cries stopped. He snuggled against her, making little smacking sounds.

"Is he all right?" Wyatt stood in the doorway, his jeans pulled up over his hips.

"He's fine. Just lonesome and hungry—and wet." Her hand felt the dampness on the seat of Mikey's pajamas. "As long as you're here, could you do me a favor? His formula bottles are downstairs in the fridge. Could you warm one a little in some hot water and bring it up here?"

When he hesitated, she added, "Or I can do it if you'd rather stay here and change him."

She glanced down at Mikey, who was sucking on his fist. When she looked up again, the doorway was empty.

So much for romance. Wyatt found the bottles in the refrigerator. The prepared formula was cold. Running some hot water in a pan he set one bottle in it and waited. How warm was the blasted formula supposed to be? He could've sworn they'd unpacked a bottle warmer last night. But Leigh was still organizing things in the nursery. It could have been put away and forgotten. After all, she'd had plenty on her mind.

As he'd just learned tonight...

Was this really what she'd planned all along? Taking the job to seduce him? He found that hard to believe, but as long as he could have her in bed he wasn't complaining about her motives.

Still, he'd be smart to keep a cool head. This wouldn't be the first time a woman had tried to use him for her own purposes.

Another thing—was she right about including the baby in the family? Lord knows he'd meant well. But was ignoring an innocent child to spare his own feelings—and perhaps the baby's—the moral choice? The humane choice?

Leigh had given him a lot to think about—more than he was fit to process tonight. It was easier to dwell on what had happened at the *end* of their conversation.

Leaning against the counter, he relived those frantic moments in her bed. She'd been so sweet, so pliant and ready. And he'd been wild with the smell and taste and feel of her. The thought of having her again had him aching like a hormone-crazed high school sophomore.

He wanted her—plain and simple. Any way he could have her. But the next time he got intimate with his sexy nanny, he wanted to make sure there'd be no distractions. He wanted the time and privacy to drive her mad with pleasure.

With Chloe and the baby in the house, that was going to take some planning.

When the bottle felt lukewarm he carried it back upstairs. From the dark hall he could see through the open doorway to where Leigh sat in the rocker with Mikey cradled in her arms. Her head was bent over him, the nightlight casting her in a soft glow. She was singing, her voice so low that he could barely hear it, let alone make out the words. But the expression on her face was one of pure love.

The emotion that stirred in him had nothing to do with lust. Seeing her in that light with the baby was like looking at a Renaissance painting—beautiful and strangely moving. For a moment he stood spellbound. Then she glanced up and saw him.

"Did you bring the formula? This little guy is hungry."

"Right here." He held up the bottle. "But I don't know if it's the right temperature."

"You test it like this." She held out her free hand, palm up. "Dribble a few drops on my wrist.... Yes, that's it. It feels about right." She gazed up at him. "Why don't you try feeding Mikey?"

Wyatt caught the challenge in her eyes. He didn't relish the idea. But something told him he'd be smart to stay on this woman's good side.

"Here, sit down." Before he could argue, she moved

out of the chair and might have shoved him into it if he hadn't taken the seat on his own. The next thing he knew the baby was in his arms. Mikey was dressed in clean yellow pajamas and wrapped in a fresh receiving blanket printed with ducklings. The eyes that gazed up at Wyatt were so pure and clear that they seemed to see into the depths of his soul.

Leigh lowered herself to the stool at his feet. "Prop him up a little. Then just brush his lips with the nipple. He'll do the rest."

Wyatt followed her suggestion. Mikey latched on to the rubber nipple as though it was the real thing. He drank with small gulping sounds, his eyes closing with pleasure. "Ease him off a little," Leigh cautioned. "You've seen what can happen if he drinks too fast. That's it...."

She was smiling up at him, the night-light soft on her face. Wyatt cursed under his breath. Damn it, but she was beautiful.

"It's a shame you don't have children of your own," he said, making conversation. "You strike me as a natural."

"Maybe someday." She glanced down at her clasped hands. "Wyatt, what happened tonight...I'm aware that I made the first move. And I can't say I didn't enjoy it. But it wasn't very smart—especially with Chloe in the house."

Wyatt nodded, reluctant to speak and startle Mikey, now a warm, sleepy bundle of contentment in his arms.

"We can't be sneaking around behind her back, hoping she won't overhear us or walk in on us," Leigh continued. "My main reason for being here is to give Mikey a loving start, and to help Chloe any way I can. None of that will work if she can't trust me."

"So what about your so-called crush?"

"Oh, it's still there." She gave him a hint of a smile. "But it might have to wait for a better time. I've been burned before, and I know better than to think either one of us is looking for a serious relationship. We had a good time, and I certainly wouldn't mind a return engagement. But first things first."

Wyatt looked down at his sleeping grandson. Mikey's eyes were closed, his lashes golden feather spikes against his rosy cheeks. Leigh was right. What mattered most was doing the right thing for Chloe and for this precious new life. Other concerns could wait.

But not forever. True, after doing the marriage thing once, Wyatt knew he wasn't husband material, or even long-term boyfriend material. But the chemistry with Leigh was too delicious to put on hold for long. He meant to get her to himself—and he wasn't a patient man.

Leigh woke to the sound of a car backing down the drive. She flew to the window to see the Bentley swing onto the road and disappear behind the trees. She glanced at the clock. Six-thirty, not even sunup. Did Wyatt have pressing business this early or was he running away from pressures on the home front?

After feeding Mikey last night, he'd made his excuses and gone downstairs. She'd known better than to go after him. He'd had an emotional day and so had she. And they could hardly spend the night together with Chloe in the house. His distance from her had only been sensible. But today was different. Wyatt had gone off and left her to deal with the teen on her own—a whole new set of challenges.

Mikey was awake in the nursery making little cooing noises in his crib. Flinging on her robe, she hurried through the connecting doorway. His eyes brightened as she leaned over to pick him up. "Hello, big boy." She kissed the soft curve of his neck, inhaling the sweet baby aroma she'd already come to love. His diaper was soaked. He'd need changing and sponging before she went downstairs. Putting him back in the crib she pulled on her jeans and a fresh shirt. By the time she'd brushed her teeth and hair he was crying. Probably hungry. Maybe she should feed him first, then get him cleaned up.

Leigh was beginning to understand why some new mothers looked so frazzled. She felt like a wreck, and she hadn't even given birth.

The soggy diaper couldn't wait. She used a wipe on his bottom, being careful to keep his cord dry, and taped a fresh disposable into place. That done, she zipped him into dry pajamas, put him in his carrier and took him down to the kitchen. He was fussing and sucking on his fist. The poor little guy was really hungry.

She put a bottle in hot water and snuggled him while she waited. When she had a minute she would find that bottle warmer she'd put somewhere. And while she was at it, she'd organize the whole process of making formula. For the sake of her own sanity, she needed to become more efficient.

She'd just begun feeding Mikey when Chloe wandered into the kitchen. Dressed in her blue sweats, she was tousled and yawning but still managed to look pretty. "What's to eat?" she mumbled, sitting down.

Leigh glanced up from feeding the baby. "Tell me what sounds good and I'll do my best."

"French toast—with bacon. I'm starved."

Leigh had seen bread, eggs, bacon and some condiments in the fridge. "That sounds doable. Take your boy. By the time you've finished feeding him, I should have it ready."

Something akin to panic flashed in Chloe's cornflower eyes. "That's all right. I can wait till you're done."

Leigh knew she couldn't back off now. "You didn't feed him in the hospital?" she asked.

She shook her russet curls. "I told the nurses I wanted to rest. I've never fed him. I thought that was your job."

"It is. But I'll eventually have a day off. If you really want to keep this baby, you need to know how to take care of him when I'm not here. Feeding him's easy. Your father did it last night."

"Daddy fed Mikey?"

Leigh nodded. "If he can do it, anybody can. Here, take him." She held the baby toward the girl.

"What if I do it wrong? What if I hurt him?" Chloe shrank away, eyes wide with what appeared to be genuine fear.

"What is it, Chloe?" Nestling Mikey against her once more, Leigh took a seat at the table. "Why did you decide to keep your baby if you don't want to take care of him?"

Tears welled in the girl's eyes. "I wanted something to love, something that was all mine. Before he was born, loving him was easy. But now that he's here, he's so little and helpless, I don't know what to do with him. I'm so scared…."

"But you're his mother. Why should you be scared?"

Chloe stared down at her hands. The nails, bitten to the quick, were painted baby-blue. "I don't know. But I remember something that happened when I was little. Mom took me to see my aunt, who'd just had a baby girl. She was so pretty, like a little doll. While Mom and Aunt Trudy were talking I tried to pick her up. I…dropped her on the hard floor. She wasn't moving. Mom called the paramedics."

"Oh, no! Was she all right?"

"She was, after a trip to the hospital. But I was so scared. I remember my aunt screaming at me, 'If she dies, it'll be your fault! Don't you ever touch a baby again!'"

"Oh, Chloe!" Leigh could have wept. What an awful thing for a girl to live with—and then to have a baby of her own while she was still too young to have the confidence to overcome the past. If she wanted Chloe to be comfortable with Mikey, she would have to take things slowly.

Mikey's bottle was almost empty. "I'll tell you what," she said. "I'll burp him, and then you can sit and hold him while I make breakfast. After that you can watch me sponge bathe him and choose a cute outfit for him to wear. Okay?"

"Okay. I think." She still looked hesitant. Leigh finished burping the baby and placed him gently in Chloe's arms. Chloe held him as if he were made of porcelain. But when he looked up at her and cooed, she smiled.

"Hi, Mikey," she whispered. "Hey, I'm your mom. How about that?"

Seven

Wyatt had weighed the wisdom of leaving Leigh to deal with Chloe by herself. In the end he'd decided to spend a busy day at the resort.

True, it was the coward's way out. But he had his reasons. He and Chloe tended to rub each other the wrong way, especially when she wasn't feeling well. Without him around, Leigh's day might be more agreeable. Besides, it was Wednesday. For years he'd made it a tradition to spend Wednesdays in his office at the Wolf Ridge Lodge. While he was there any resort employee, from the managers to the lowliest dishwasher, could drop by to air a grievance, ask a question or make a suggestion. The practice paid dividends in efficiency and employee morale. It also got him out of the house while the cleaning crew did their work.

But today Wyatt's thoughts weren't just on business. The memory of Leigh in his arms was a smoldering reminder of where he wanted to take this relationship. She'd been right about the pitfalls of a secret affair while Chloe was in the house. Sooner or later the girl was bound to find out. And the discovery that her father was sleeping with the nanny would be a calamity for all concerned.

But there had to be ways around that. After all, he owned a resort with a hotel. The trick would be getting Leigh out of the house for a night. Between her duties with Mikey and Chloe's raised eyebrows, that was going to be a challenge. But Wyatt had never been one to let difficulties stand in his way. Somehow he would manage this. He wanted some leisurely time to make love to Leigh. And one way or another, he would find it.

He might not be good for the long haul. But at least he knew how to make a woman happy in bed.

"I'm bored!" Chloe flipped through the TV channels and tossed the remote on the floor. "Why can't I go out with my friends?"

"It's Wednesday. Your friends are in school." Leigh glanced up from folding the basket of baby clothes she'd just laundered. "Maybe you can have them here this weekend. Why don't you ask your father when he gets home?"

"He'll say no. He wants to keep me locked up like a prisoner."

"That's nonsense. He wants to keep you and Mikey safe, that's all."

"Well, I don't need protecting. I'm going crazy in this house. And I don't have anything to wear! I want to go shopping!"

Leigh sighed. "Give it time, Chloe. Your body's still getting back to normal. Besides, it's probably too soon to take Mikey out. He could get sick."

Muttering, Chloe dragged herself off the sofa and wandered down the stairs. She was probably going to spend some time on the computer in her room. Would Wyatt's security team be monitoring her internet activity? But that was Wyatt's problem, Leigh reminded herself. She'd made it clear she wasn't going to police the girl.

Mikey had gone down for his nap an hour ago. Soon he'd be awake and needing attention. Leigh brushed a stray lock out of her eyes. Her nephew was a precious angel, but tending to his needs was wearing her down.

Chloe hadn't moved much beyond holding him. When she'd watched Leigh bathe the baby, she'd taken one look at the shriveling umbilical cord and declared that it was "gross." Maybe Wyatt had the right idea. Chloe still had so much growing up to do—was it fair to Mikey to keep him from an adoptive mother who'd be better prepared to give him everything he needed? But it was too soon to give up. In spite of her immaturity, Leigh could see that Chloe truly did love her baby. For the sake of everyone involved, Leigh knew she had to keep trying.

From Chloe's room, rap music blasted up the stairs. The noise was loud enough to wake Mikey. Hearing him fuss, Leigh raced down the hall to the nursery. She'd just picked him up when the front doorbell rang.

Tucking the baby into her arms, she made her way downstairs to the entry. As the bell jangled a second time, she reached the door and cautiously opened it.

A middle-aged woman stood on the front porch with two young men behind her. All three were dressed in maroon and silver Wolf Ridge Resort uniforms, complete with ID badges.

"Cleaning crew." The woman was short and huskily built, with wiry gray curls and a smile that lit her round moon of a face. The smile broadened as she caught sight of the baby. "So that's the little man! Hello there, Mr. Mikey!"

Leigh's jaw dropped. Clearly the woman had been talking to Wyatt. "Please come in and get started," she said, stepping back. "We'll do our best to stay out of your way."

"No, it's our job to stay out of *your* way." The woman stepped inside and motioned the two younger men toward the back of the house where the cleaning supplies were kept. "My name's Dora. And since your eyes are popping out of your head, I'll explain. I've been coming here to clean this house for the past nine years. Mr. Richardson trusts me like family. And he knows I keep my mouth shut."

Glancing at the woman's badge, Leigh read the words Housekeeping Supervisor. "I'm happy to meet you, Dora," she said. "Mikey may not be at his best right now. He just woke up, and I can smell his messy diaper."

"Oh, never mind that!" Dora reached out and scooped Mikey into her arms. "I've smelled plenty of diapers. Raised four kids on my own after my husband left—all girls, and they turned out fine. Mr. Richardson says you're pretty new at this. Would you like my phone number? You can call me anytime you have a question about babies."

"Thank you." Leigh felt as if she'd been drowning and the woman had tossed her a life preserver. "I really mean that. I just hope I won't bother you too much."

"No such thing as too much." Dora lifted Mikey to eye level, making little clucking sounds as she bounced him in her arms. Young as he was, Mikey responded, cooing in unmistakable delight. "Look at this handsome boy," she murmured. "And those blue Richardson eyes! This one's going to break hearts, just like his grandpa!"

She broke off, as if realizing she'd said too much. In the stillness Leigh could hear the two young men cleaning the kitchen.

"Where's the new mother?" Dora asked.

The rap music blaring from the hallway answered her question. Dora frowned and shook her head. "Oh, mercy, this won't do."

The next thing Leigh knew, Dora was striding down the hall with Mikey in the crook of her arm. Her free hand knocked sharply on Chloe's door.

The music stopped. Seconds passed before the door opened.

"Here you are, Miss Chloe," Dora said. "Since your so-called music woke this baby, he's all yours—and right now he needs his diaper changed."

Chloe's pert nose wrinkled. "That's not my job. It's the nanny's."

Dora's scowl deepened. "You're his mother. A nanny's job is to *help* you, not take your place." She glanced back at Leigh, who was watching wide-eyed. "Miss Foster, if you wouldn't mind bringing us some clean diapers and wipes, and maybe a towel."

The woman's voice rang with authority. Leigh raced to the nursery and returned with what was needed. Dora, who'd raised four girls, was giving her a lesson in how to handle a surly teen mother—a lesson Leigh badly needed to learn.

"Daddy, I changed Mikey's diapers today."

"Oh?" Wyatt glanced up from his plate of braised chicken, potatoes and gravy.

"They were gross. But I did it. I gave him a bottle, too."

"That's nice."

Sitting across the candlelit dinner table, Leigh glanced from father to daughter. Chloe seemed to crave her father's approval. But Wyatt was too preoccupied to notice. Seeing Chloe's disappointment at his nonresponse, Leigh thought of praising the girl herself, but decided against it. Dora had told her not to make too much of a fuss over Chloe for helping with Mikey's care—the teenager needed to see tending her baby as part of her normal routine, not something deserving special recognition.

Dora had made more progress with Chloe than Leigh had believed possible. In past years she'd served as Chloe's babysitter and was firmly in charge. Chloe had obeyed her without a murmur of argument.

Leigh felt she'd gained a friend as well, someone she could turn to when she needed advice. Dora had already given her some helpful hints on getting Mikey to sleep and organizing his things for more efficiency. His portable bassinet was now in Chloe's room, along with extra diapers, wipes and pajama outfits.

Dora was bound to know a lot about Wyatt. But Leigh had known better than to bring him up. The woman's first loyalty would be to her boss. Discussing his personal life would cross a forbidden line.

Leigh watched the play of candlelight on his rugged features. Remembering their plunge into passion the night before, a slow heat stirred inside her. Despite their constraints, she was eager for the next time. But tonight he seemed withdrawn. Maybe he was accustomed to sex partners who were gone the next morning. A woman who was waiting when he came home to dinner might be too much of an intrusion into his life.

"I'm having a new car delivered tomorrow," Wyatt said. "It's a Mercedes SUV with all-wheel drive and good snow tires. Leigh, it's to be your transportation while you're here. You can use it for errands and to drive Chloe and the baby where they need to go."

Chloe's fork clattered to the table. "What about me? Where's my sports car?"

Wyatt sighed. "You can't drive a sports car on these roads in wintertime, Chloe. Besides, I have yet to see that driver's license you told me you had."

"I know how to drive!" Chloe snapped.

"Maybe you do. But without that license, you're not getting behind the wheel."

Chloe's lower lip jutted outward in a little girl pout. "That's not fair, Daddy. I never finished driver training because I got pregnant and had to quit school. But Mom let me drive anyway. Ask her. I can drive just fine!"

"Not without your license, young lady. There should be a copy of the driver's handbook online. After you've studied it, you can go and take your test."

"And then you'll buy me a sports car?"

"We'll see—in the spring when the snow's gone."

"No! You promised! Two years ago, you said—" She broke off as she met his steely eyes. "Forget it! I can't believe anything you say!"

Bolting out of her chair, she stormed down the hall. The slam of her bedroom door reverberated through the house, waking Mikey in his upstairs crib.

"I'll get him." Leigh jumped up from the table and darted toward the stairs. Chloe had made a lot of progress today, but she was still sixteen years old, teetering between maturity and childhood.

Wyatt watched her rush out of sight. With a weary exhalation he pushed away his half-finished dinner. The clash with Chloe had pretty much destroyed his appetite. He was trying to do right by the girl. Why did she have to test him at every turn?

And what about Leigh? She'd told him she wanted Chloe to bond with her baby. But it was his lovely nanny who seemed to be doing most of the bonding. She couldn't be more attached to the little boy if she'd given birth to him herself. What would she do when the time came to let Mikey go?

Thinking of that sweet, innocent infant nestling in his arms last night, he found he was uncomfortable with the thought of Mikey leaving, too. And not just because he didn't know what he'd do when Leigh no longer had a reason to stay in his home.

Leigh returned moments later with Mikey snuggled against her shoulder. He was chomping hungrily on the collar of her shirt. "I think he wants his bottle," she said. "Do you mind holding him while I warm it?"

"Not a bit." Wyatt held out his arms for the baby. It amazed him how fast he was getting used to the little fellow. Holding him now seemed as natural as breathing.

Mikey was no longer fussing. His clear gaze took Wyatt in. Wyatt had heard somewhere that newborns couldn't focus their eyes. But in Mikey's case he didn't believe it. Those big blues seemed to be seeing everything.

"Hello, Mikey," he said using the gruff voice the baby seemed to like. "How's your day been? Want to tell me about it?"

Expressions flickered like sunbeams across the tiny face—surprise, amazement, a fearsome scowl—or was Mikey just passing gas? Wyatt found himself wondering what the boy would be like in years to come. Would he take to skiing? Would he be quick to learn in school? Would the girls chase after him?

But if things went as planned, he would never know, Wyatt reminded himself. How could Chloe raise a child when she was still a child herself?

Leigh had brought the bottle warmer downstairs and was waiting for the formula to heat. She stood by the kitchen counter, watching him with the baby. The tenderness in her eyes almost did him in. But it was little Mikey who'd put it there, he'd told himself. Even though they'd had a great time in bed, she had no reason to look at her grumpy, over-the-hill employer with so much love.

Face it, he wasn't good at relationships. Building a business, making money and providing generously for those in his care—that had been his way of showing love, the only way he knew how. The rest of it—the tenderness, the involvement, the sharing of time and emotion, was like a closed door to him.

"Mikey is so contented with you," she said. "You've got just the right touch."

He had to say it. "You're wrong, Leigh. I've been a decent provider. But when it comes to nurturing, I haven't got a clue. Experience has taught me that I just don't have what it takes to be a family man."

"I'm not sure I believe that. Look at you." Testing the formula on her wrist, Leigh walked back toward the table. Just watching her move was a pleasure. The sway of her jeans-clad hips and the flowing stride of her long legs teased his senses. Wyatt imagined her gliding naked across a candlelit room, the soft glow bathing her skin, her delicious breasts rising and falling with each breath, while he lay on his bed, waiting for her....

Damn, this wasn't helping!

"Since you're holding Mikey, would you like to feed him?"

Had she heard a word of what he'd just told her? Or was she trying to convince him he was wrong? Wyatt shook his head. "You can have him back. But I can't believe how much he changes from day to day. Tonight he's really been looking me over."

Leigh's breast brushed the peak of his ear as she reached past him to lift the baby. Choosing a nearby chair, she settled him in her arms and offered him the bottle. Mikey took it like a pro. She smiled.

"I'm remembering something Dora said—that Mikey seems to be one of those babies who come into the world knowing just how to get on with their lives. She called him an old soul."

Wyatt tried to ignore the tightness in his throat. "Dora's a gem," he said.

"She truly is. I can't believe how well she handled Chloe."

"Yes. Chloe." Wyatt exhaled. "Tonight you got a glimpse of her dark side. After seeing that little tantrum, do you still think the girl is ready to be a mother?"

"I never said she was," Leigh replied gently. "But she's capable of loving her baby and taking some responsibility for him. You should have seen her after she changed his diaper and fed him. She was so proud of herself. But when she told you about it tonight, all you said was 'That's nice.' It was like you hadn't even heard her."

"Maybe I didn't know what else to say. Am I supposed to be proud that my sixteen-year-old daughter can change and feed her—" He bit back the ugly, unthinkable word.

"Oh, Wyatt!" Her stricken look was like an ice pick in his chest. "She's still your little girl. And right now you're all she's got. She wants to know that you're on her side, that you believe in her. She needs you—and she loves you."

"She's got a funny way of showing it."

"I'm guessing it's the only way she knows." Leigh glanced down at the baby, then back at Wyatt. Her eyes were amber in the light of the burning candle. "I was about Chloe's age when I lost my father in a plane crash. We'd had an argument that morning because he wouldn't let me go to a party. As he went out the door with his suitcase the last words I said to him were 'I hate you.'"

The emotion in her voice was so wrenching that Wyatt couldn't reply.

"Of course I didn't mean it. And I have to think he knew that. But over the years…" She shook her head. "I'd give anything, even now, to have him back long enough to tell him I love him."

Wyatt found his voice. "Have you told Chloe that story?"

"I've never told anyone. Not until tonight."

His gaze caressed her—the softness of her features, the glimmer of tears in her eyes, the stray lock of dark hair that fell across her face. He'd known some stunning women in his time. But Leigh was beautiful to the marrow of her bones.

She glanced down at Mikey, as if overcome by sudden regret. Was she sorry she'd been so open with him?

For the flicker of a moment he was tempted to tell her about his own father. But he'd never shared that part of his past with anyone. And the story was so ugly it would only repel her. What he really wanted right now was to get her into his arms—and his bed—again. There, he'd know exactly what to do, exactly how to please her. But that would have to wait for a better time and place.

Since she was holding the baby, he had to settle for rising, stepping behind her and placing his hands on her shoulders. His thumbs gently massaged the tension from her taut muscles. She responded with a little purring sound that triggered wicked images in his mind.

"Thank you," he said, reining in his thoughts. "It means a lot, your sharing that story. It helps me put Chloe's issues in perspective."

"I wasn't so different myself at that age. I had to grow up fast after my father died. Chloe will grow up, too."

"I know," he said. "And I'm sure your father must've known you loved him."

Mikey stirred and began to fuss, breaking the quiet spell that had fallen over them.

"That reminds me," she said. "I haven't called my mother since I got here. I'd like to take Mikey upstairs, get him settled and phone her now, before it gets too late. Do you mind?"

"Of course not." Wyatt willed himself not to sound disappointed.

"Don't worry." She rose, still cradling Mikey in her arms. "I haven't forgotten the paper I signed. I won't disclose a thing."

He watched her turn away. Had it been overkill, asking her to sign the nondisclosure agreement? Now that he knew her, the whole idea seemed ludicrous. He could no longer imagine distrusting her. Though he still felt she was keeping something from him, he was sure it was nothing harmful or malicious—she would never do anything to hurt him or his family.

But trust wasn't the only thing on his mind as she walked toward the door. She moved like a dancer, her fluid hips whispering seduction. Wyatt cursed under his breath. Didn't the woman know what she was doing to him? If she hadn't been holding the baby, and if Chloe hadn't been nearby, he'd have been tempted to go after her, spin her against him and kiss her all the way to his bedroom. In the days before his life turned upside down that might have been possible. But Leigh was only here because Chloe and the baby were here—an irony that was driving him crazy. For now he had no choice except to wait.

Once they finally had time to explore each other thoroughly, surely this aching attraction would become manageable. The draw he felt toward her, the need to be close—nothing more than the symptoms of delayed gratification at work.

A physical relationship was all he had to offer her, so he had to believe that that was all he wanted.

Leigh changed Mikey, laid him in the crib and turned on the musical duck mobile. He wasn't sleepy but the sound and motion might at least keep him quiet while she made her phone call.

It was Kevin who answered on the second ring. "Hey, sis! How's the secret agent business? Where're you calling from, Bangladesh?"

"Silly!" Leigh made a show of laughing off his question. What would Kevin do if he knew she was less than an hour away, taking care of his baby son? "I'm just calling to check in with Mom. Is she around?"

"She's right here, fighting me for the phone—hey!" His laughter faded into the background as Leigh's mother came on.

"Is everything all right, dear?" Leigh could picture her, dressed in the black pantsuit she wore for selling real estate, her makeup in place, her chestnut hair meticulously dyed and curled. Diane Foster was a survivor, a woman who hid her vulnerability beneath the tough exterior it took to get ahead in the world.

"Everything's fine, Mom. I just wanted to say hello. How are things at home?"

"We're managing. I think I may have sold that old Meriwether house down the block. And Kevin's made the midterm honor roll. But we miss you. I just wish you could tell me more about your new job."

"So do I. But I had to sign a nondisclosure agreement. Just know that I'm safe, and I'll be in touch. As I said before, you can always reach me on my cell."

"I know. But I hate to bother—" She broke off. "Heavens to Betsy, what's that noise?"

Leigh's pulse lurched as she turned back to face the crib. For whatever reason, Mikey had started to fuss. As she leaned over him, his whimpers rose to a full-blown baby howl.

Eight

"What am I hearing?" Leigh's mother demanded again. "It sounds like a baby crying."

"It...*is* a baby." Leigh sagged against the side of the crib. A blatant lie, she knew, would make her mother even more suspicious. "I'm not supposed to tell you this, but I'm babysitting for a celebrity family. I'm not allowed to say who it is or where they are. It has to be kept a secret. You can't even tell Kevin. Is he still there with you?"

"No, he's gone up to his room."

"Good. He can't know, Mom. If he does, he might tell someone or try to find out more. If that happens, I'm out of a well-paying job."

In truth, the job was the least of her worries, but Leigh had already said more than she should.

"I understand, dear," her mother said sweetly. "Don't worry, I won't breathe a word. But I don't want to worry about you. Promise to keep in touch, all right?"

"I promise. And now I have to go. This baby needs my attention. We'll talk later, okay? Love you."

Ending the call, Leigh gathered Mikey into her arms. He stopped crying as soon as she picked him up. The little mischief clearly wanted to be held. He was already getting spoiled. Tomorrow she would ask Dora if it was all right to let him cry a little. For now she would just snuggle him. She enjoyed it as much as he seemed to.

"What's up, Mikey?" She brushed a kiss across the top of his silky head. "What do you think of the world so far? How about the people in it? Do you think we're a pretty loony bunch?"

He cooed and butted his head against her shoulder. Laughing, she pressed her nose against his neck, inhaling his clean, milky baby smell. "You're my sweet boy," she whispered. "And I love you. Never forget that."

"Lucky little man." Wyatt stood in the doorway. "What do *I* need to do for that kind of treatment?"

Leigh stifled a gasp. How long had he been there? How much had he heard?

"I hope you weren't eavesdropping," she said.

"Nothing of the kind. Just feeling the quiet a bit too much. I was about to turn on the news and wondered if you wanted to share some hot cocoa and watch it with me."

"I'll pass on the cocoa, thanks. But if you don't mind my bringing Mikey, I'll watch the news with you. Being up here is like being on the moon. I could use a reminder of the real world."

Still apprehensive, she followed him into the cozy lounge area at the top of the stairs. He'd dimmed the lights and switched on the gas-fueled fireplace. Wyatt's invitation had sounded harmless enough. But what was he up to? Did he suspect something? Did he want to pry more secrets out of her?

If only things were simpler! Aside from the complications, snuggling on the couch with Wyatt and the baby sounded like a little bit of heaven.

Still cradling Mikey, she settled against the cushions. Wyatt sat down beside her. His arm lay across the back of the couch, not quite touching her. He was probably thinking of Chloe, who could wander out of her room at any time.

Clicking the remote, he switched on a local channel. "I wanted to get the weather report," he said. "We might be getting snow—and snow is our business here. Do you ski?"

Leigh shook her head. "By the time I was old enough I had a part-time job. With that and school, there was no time to learn."

"I could give you some personal lessons."

She forced a laugh. "Trust me, I'm not the queen of co-ordination. I'd probably break something. How would I take care of Mikey, dragging around in a cast?"

"Maybe later, then." His fingertips brushed her shoulder. "The other night wasn't enough, Leigh. I want some serious time with you."

His meaning was clear. Leigh glanced down at Mikey, fearful that Wyatt might read the truth in her face. She craved the chance for more intimacy with him. But every encounter would raise the risk she was taking. If he were to learn the truth, he'd want nothing more to do with her.

"Leigh? Have I misread some signals?"

She forced herself to meet his gaze. Golden flames reflected in the blue depths of his eyes. She remembered those eyes blazing down at her in the lamplight of her bedroom as he filled her with his heat. Wyatt's lovemaking had made her want to beg for more. But would deepening their involvement only lead to more bitterness in the end?

She shook her head, willing herself to be as honest as she dared. "You haven't misread anything, Wyatt. I'd welcome more time together if we could find it. But things are a bit…overwhelming right now. I have all I can handle with Mikey and Chloe."

"Fine. For now…but not for long, Leigh. As you know, I'm not a patient man." Tilting her chin with a finger he brushed a feathery kiss across her lips. The brief contact sent a jolt of sensual need through her body. She ached with wanting him—his arms around her, his skin naked against hers. But was she willing to risk the consequences?

Mikey made a little whimpering sound, like a puppy wanting attention. Reaching out, Wyatt nudged the baby's hand. The tiny fist closed around his finger and held on tight. He laughed.

"He's a precious little guy, isn't he? I can see why you've become so attached to him."

Leigh braced herself for a lecture on why Chloe shouldn't keep her baby. But the weather forecast had come on the TV. With Mikey still clasping his finger, Wyatt gave it his full attention.

By the time the forecast ended, he was grinning like a schoolboy. "Snow! Not a big storm but maybe enough to open early—even if we have to bring out the snow machines. And it's already moving in. What do you say to that, Mikey?"

But Mikey had fallen asleep in Leigh's arms.

Easing his finger free, Wyatt gazed down at his slumbering grandson. "He's beautiful, isn't he?"

"Yes. I see a lot of Chloe in him. And now that he's asleep, maybe I can put him back to bed." Fighting emotion, she rose with the baby and turned away.

"Leigh." His voice caught her as she moved toward the hall.

"Is there something you need?"

"Yes. After you've put him down, come back."

Leigh retreated without a reply. Coming back to him could open the door to disaster. She'd be a fool to trust herself with the man. But deeper instincts told her that nothing could keep her away.

Mikey was sound asleep. He didn't even whimper as she laid him on his back. All the same, she lingered beside the crib, watching him as she battled the urge to race back to Wyatt—a battle she had no wish to win.

She could no longer hear the TV. Had he given up on waiting and gone downstairs? Pulse racing, she hurried back to where she'd left him. The lights and TV were off and the couch was empty.

She was about to turn and go back to her room when the door to the balcony opened and Wyatt walked in. His cobalt eyes were sparkling, his cheeks flushed with cold. "Come outside with me. You've got to see this," he said.

Lifting a knitted afghan from the back of the couch, he held it like a wrap. "Come on. This'll keep you warm. Now close your eyes."

Enfolded in the thick wool, Leigh allowed him to lead her out through the door. Shutting it behind them, he led her to the rail. "Now look!" he said.

Leigh opened her eyes. It was snowing—a world of fluffy, white flakes drifting down through the darkness. Far below, veiled by snowfall, she could see the lights of the resort. But here where they stood, snow and darkness were all around them. "It's magical," she whispered. "Like being in the middle of a giant Christmas card!"

His laugh tickled her ear as he drew her close. And then he was kissing her—with tender passion, the way she'd always dreamed of being kissed. She stretched on tiptoe, responding to the night, the snow and the fairy-tale kiss that went on and on.

Heaven save her, was she falling in love?

* * *

Two weeks had passed. Mikey was growing every day, becoming more alert and even more adorable. Mikey's mother, however, was climbing the walls. Chloe's strong young body had made a remarkable recovery from the birth. She was squeezing herself into her old jeans and clamoring for a trip to town, to buy new clothes and hang out with her friends.

Wyatt, who'd been spending most of his time at the resort, had turned a deaf ear to her constant whining. Only after Leigh took the girl's side and offered to drive her had he given in. Even then, he'd insisted that Leigh keep an eye on his daughter and have her back by dinnertime.

Mikey was to be left home. Wyatt had arranged for Dora to tend him, but she'd come down with a cold at the last minute. In the wake of Chloe's tears, Wyatt had agreed to take time from the resort and watch the boy himself. He had plenty to do, but he could always work from his office while the baby slept.

Standing on the balcony, with Mikey swathed in blankets, he watched the Mercedes vanish behind the trees. It was time to let Chloe go out, he told himself. The girl needed some freedom and he couldn't protect her forever. But it felt strange, being left here with the baby. He could have asked one of his other employees to come. But there was no one other than Dora who he trusted alone in the house with his precious grandson.

Chloe, during one of her rants, had accused him of being overprotective. And he supposed he was. But there were people on the outside who wouldn't stop at exploiting his family or even harming them. He wanted—needed—to keep them safe. In spite of his plans not to get attached, Mikey was on that list.

And what about Leigh? Standing on the spot where he'd

last kissed her, Wyatt felt the familiar yearning. Between his work, her work and family pressures, time alone with her had become a rare commodity. A tender glance across the table, a brush of hands when passing on the stairs… Damn, it was better than nothing. But it wasn't enough. He wanted her in his arms, in his bed. And he was losing patience.

He could only hope Leigh was, too.

Mikey stirred, fussing in his arms. He'd just awakened and wasn't likely to nap anytime soon. Wyatt brushed a kiss across the russet curls. "Hey, big guy," he murmured. "What do you say we go inside and watch some football?"

While Leigh drove, Chloe texted, her thumbs a blur of movement over the face of her cell phone. Wyatt's daughter was excited to see her friends, and a Saturday afternoon with them at the mall was probably her idea of heaven.

It would be Leigh's job to tag along at a discreet distance and pretend she wasn't really with them. Chloe had her own credit card and could buy whatever struck her fancy. Her friends, all from well-off families, probably had the same.

For teens, the new Dutchman's Creek Mall was the social center of town. Chloe's three friends were waiting by the fountain inside the main entrance. They raced toward her, squealing and jumping up and down as they came together. Standing back, Leigh felt like an aging duenna. Fragments of conversation drifted to her ears—boys, dates, clothes and a little about the baby. Chloe had never seemed happier. Maybe it was time Wyatt thought about sending his daughter back to the exclusive private school she'd attended last year. Leigh resolved to mention it the next time they had a chance to talk.

Not that those chances came often. Wyatt was very

much a hands-on owner. With the resort opening early, he was busy from morning to night checking the equipment, interviewing new staff and seeing that everything was in perfect order. She remembered what Chloe had told her on the way home that first day—that Wyatt was generous with money and things, but not with his time. Now she understood the truth of that. How could any woman compete with his work?

Leigh had seen so little of him that she'd begun to wonder if she'd imagined that breathless kiss in the snow. But then, she'd been equally busy with Chloe and Mikey.

Still, the work hadn't kept her from dreaming up some luscious fantasies....

Chloe's friends were crowding around her, exclaiming over the baby photos on her cell phone. It pleased Leigh to see that she'd snapped some. Unprepared as the girl was to be a mother, she did appear to love her little boy. The question of giving up Mikey was no longer being asked. Even Wyatt had stopped mentioning it.

Laughing and chattering, the four girls headed into the main part of the mall. Leigh kept pace with them, hovering as they trooped into exclusive shops to try on the kind of clothes she hadn't even dreamed of wearing as a teen. Chloe's purchases—two cashmere sweaters, a leather jacket, designer jeans, boots, a five-hundred dollar purse, and several sets of panties and bras, went into shopping bags. Leigh, who'd offered to carry them, was soon loaded down like a pack animal. She was grateful she'd worn her walking shoes, but she was getting tired.

Ahead of them, the sounds and smells of the food court drifted down the mall. "Who's hungry?" Chloe demanded. "Burgers and shakes for everybody, my treat!"

Like a flock of colorful birds, the girls circled and descended on a corner table. A snap of Chloe's fingers summoned a waiter. Wyatt's daughter was clearly in her element. "Want anything, Leigh?" she asked.

"Just a Coke, thanks." Leigh seated herself in a nearby chair. Ignoring her, the girls buzzed away, laughing and checking their phones for text messages. Tuning them out for the moment, Leigh rested her feet and let her thoughts drift back to Wyatt. Today was the first time he'd taken care of Mikey alone. By now he seemed at ease with his tiny grandson; but what if something unplanned were to happen? Could he handle it?

A hush had fallen over the girls' table. Following their gazes, Leigh saw three nice-looking high school boys strolling into the far end of the food court.

Her heart dropped.

One of them was Kevin.

Wyatt had moved the bassinet from Chloe's room to his office and set it on the floor by his desk. After feeding Mikey a warm bottle, he laid him on his back, tucked a blanket over his legs, and switched on his computer. With luck, the baby would sleep for several hours, allowing him to get some needed planning done for the resort. In this busy season, he couldn't spare time away from work.

He'd just brought up the spreadsheet for the restaurant when Mikey started to whimper. Remembering Leigh's mention that he sometimes fussed before going to sleep, Wyatt willed himself to ignore the little fellow. But as minutes passed, the cries became more insistent. Turning in his chair, he looked down. The small, tear-streaked face tore at his heart.

"What is it, Mikey? Are you okay?"

At the sound of his voice, Mikey's cries grew louder. Giving in to the inevitable, Wyatt picked the baby up and lifted him against his shoulder. Usually being held was all he wanted. But this time Mikey kept on crying. His body was rigid, as if he were in pain.

"What is it, big guy?" Wyatt rubbed the bony little back, growing more worried by the minute. Maybe he should call Dora and ask her what to do.

He was reaching for the phone when Mikey gave a little hiccup and spit a stream of sour formula down Wyatt's shoulder. Only then did Wyatt remember he hadn't burped the baby before putting him down. Spitting up seemed to take care of the problem. He'd stopped crying and was gazing at Wyatt with those dazzling eyes.

"If you could talk, I suppose you'd say this served me right!" Wyatt muttered. Rising, he carried Mikey into his room and laid him on a towel while he changed his shirt. Mikey's pajamas hadn't escaped the mess, and his diaper smelled suspiciously rank. He would need changing, too.

Upstairs in the nursery Wyatt managed to get his grandson out of his dirty clothes, wipe him down and dress him again. Mikey seemed to enjoy the process, cooing and kicking his feet the whole time. "You know, for such a little fellow, you're a lot of work," Wyatt said. "But something tells me you're here to stay."

As he spoke the words, Wyatt knew he meant them. This baby had become part of the family, and he would do everything in his power to help Chloe raise him. And maybe this time, he could take a more active role. He had to set an example for Chloe, and with Leigh there to make sure he got everything right, he might be able to handle being a good parental figure after all.

Looking down at the happy baby, he felt the now-familiar tightening in his chest. Something told him it was love.

Kevin and his friends John and Mark had paused in the entrance to the food court and were surveying the place, maybe looking for friends. Seized by panic, Leigh ducked her head and nudged Chloe's shoulder. "Going to the restroom," she whispered. "Keep an eye on your bags."

Chloe paid her scant attention as she slunk off, weaving among the crowded tables in an effort to keep her back to the boys. She hated to leave the girl unawares, but there was no way to warn Chloe without giving herself away. She could only hope Kevin wouldn't notice the mother of his child, sitting across the food court with her girlfriends.

But what chance was there of that, when Chloe's flame-hued curls stood out like a beacon? Leigh reached the open L-shaped entrance to the ladies' room and flattened herself inside the barrier wall. Peering around it, she could see most of the food court. The boys were moving in the direction of the table, the girls watching them, giggling with anticipation—all except for Chloe. She sat frozen, staring down at her clenched hands. If only Leigh could have rescued the poor girl from her awkward situation. But there was nothing she could do without giving herself away.

The boys passed the entrance to the ladies' room, so close that Leigh could almost have reached out and touched her brother. They were moving on when Kevin halted as if he'd slammed into an invisible wall.

"Hey, man, what's wrong?" Mark asked.

"Nothing. Just remembered something I need to do for my mom." Kevin sounded as if he'd seen a ghost.

"Now? When we're about to go talk to those hot girls?"

"You two go on. I'll call you later." Kevin did an about-face and strode hastily out of the food court, the way the boys had come in.

His two friends stared after him. "What was that all about?" John asked. Mark just shrugged.

Leigh began to breathe again. But she still wasn't out of the woods. Kevin's two friends had been to their house.

They would recognize her, too. What if they joined the girls? What would she do if the bunch of them went off somewhere together?

The boys had gone a few more steps toward the girls' table when Mark stopped with a muttered oath. "Hey, I know those chicks. They go to Bramford Hill. They're so snooty rich they won't even talk to common trash like us. Let's go before they put us down. We'll have better luck someplace else."

Leigh sagged against the wall in relief as the boys turned and left. She'd come so close to having everything blow up in her face—Kevin, Chloe, the baby…and Wyatt, who'd never speak to her again unless it was in court.

This time she'd had a narrow escape. But in many ways Dutchman's Creek was still a small town. There were bound to be more encounters, and next time she might not be so lucky. There was no getting around it—sooner or later the truth would come out. And when it did, the consequences would crush her.

Nine

By early November the snow was four feet deep on the runs. Wyatt had hoped for more but, with the help of the snow machines, there was enough to start the season. The lodge and hotel were booked, the restaurants and shops teeming with visitors.

Things were calm enough on the home front, as well. Mikey was growing into a robust, bright-eyed cherub. Chloe had started some online classes and would be going back to school spring semester, after the worst of the snow was gone. Meanwhile, she'd wheedled a promise from her father that during Christmas vacation she could have her friends up to the house for a ski holiday.

But as for Leigh…

Wyatt stood on the balcony gazing out at the leaden sky. The weather matched his mood. Ever since her trip with Chloe to the Dutchman's Creek Mall, he'd sensed a cooling in her demeanor toward him. She almost seemed to be avoiding him. Something had happened, and he didn't know what it was.

The frustration did nothing to dampen his desire. If anything, it made him want her even more. When misunderstandings or mixed messages had gotten between him and women before, he'd always worked it out in bed. He was confident he could do the same with Leigh, if they could just find an opportunity. There was no way he was going to let this woman escape without some serious lovemaking. He'd already waited too long. It was time he made his move.

One way or another, before the week was out, he was determined to get his beautiful nanny in bed. At the moment, she'd opted to visit her family for a couple of days. Some time off was written into her contract and she was ready for a change of scene. Wednesday night she'd be back.

She'd planned on driving her station wagon, which was in storage at the resort. But Wyatt had insisted she take the new Mercedes SUV. The canyon roads were slick with snow and he wanted her safe. Or maybe he was worried that she'd take her old rust bucket and disappear for good.

"What are you doing out here, Daddy? It's cold." Chloe stood in the doorway. Her sweet-as-pie smile told him she had a favor to ask. Steeling himself, he followed her inside and sat down.

"Tell me, have I been a good girl?" she asked. "Have I done my schoolwork and taken care of Mikey with Leigh gone?"

"You have." His eyebrow quirked. "I do believe there's hope for you yet."

She giggled charmingly. "Well, here's the thing, Daddy. Friday's Monique's birthday, and she's having a slumber party at her house. All my girlfriends will be there. Leigh won't even have to drive me. Amy says she can pick me up and bring me home the next day. Please say I can go."

She looked as appealing as a puppy. Wyatt had to admit she'd earned a break. "You can go on one condition," he said. "I want to make sure Monique's parents will be there to keep an eye on things. Give me their phone number and I'll make the call."

"Thank you, Daddy! You're the best! I'll text Monique and get the number for you." She jumped up, gave him a peck on the cheek and raced down the stairs to her room.

Watching her go, Wyatt felt a prickle of uncertainty that made him want to retract his permission. Maybe he was being overprotective. But this was a girl who'd had unprotected sex after a bout of underage drinking and Lord knows what else. He couldn't be too careful.

Then again, Chloe did deserve a treat…and besides, he couldn't ignore that other voice in his head—the one reminding him that, with Chloe gone overnight, he might finally get some time alone with Leigh. The timing of the annual winter reception gave him the perfect excuse to ask her out. If he could arrange for Dora to tend Mikey overnight, he could put the rest of his plan in motion.

He kept a secluded room at the lodge where he could stay if he needed to work late. The well-appointed suite also came in handy for entertaining female guests. Now, as he pictured the sitting room with its adjoining bed-chamber, he realized it wasn't what he wanted for Leigh.

Too many memories, for one thing. Women from college students to models and movie stars had shared that bed over the years. Something told him Leigh would know, and it wouldn't bode well for setting a romantic mood. Even though they'd agreed that they weren't looking for a long-term relationship together, Leigh deserved better than to be treated like another one-night stand. He wanted a special setting—no, a perfect setting, the best that money could buy.

Adjacent to the rustic-style lodge was a fifteen-story luxury hotel. Much of the topmost floor was taken up by a penthouse suite complete with a hot tub on the terrace, a private elevator and a glorious view of the mountains. Reserved for visiting celebrities, royals and millionaires, the suite rented for ten thousand dollars a night.

As the owner, he would have no problem reserving the suite. He wanted Leigh to be impressed. Even more, he wanted her to know how important she was to him. And he wanted to make glorious, unbridled love to her in a sumptuous place where they wouldn't be disturbed.

Leigh had taken her mother to lunch while Kevin was in school. That night the three of them had devoured a pizza and seen a movie at the nearby dollar theater. The mall had a megaplex showing all the current releases. But Leigh had made excuses not to go there. Better not to risk running into Chloe's friends.

She was beginning to feel like a fugitive.

Her mother and brother had been curious about the expensive car. But it was easy enough to explain that she'd borrowed it from her employer. When Kevin pumped her for more information, Leigh had simply refused to answer his questions.

Around ten o'clock, their mother went to bed, leaving the two of them alone in the kitchen. Kevin poured a tall glass of milk, added a squirt of chocolate syrup and sat down at the table. His handsome young face looked troubled.

"What is it?" Leigh asked. "You know you can tell me."

He sighed, stirring his milk with a spoon. "I should probably just forget this. But I saw Chloe a couple of weeks ago. She was at the mall with her girlfriends."

"Did you talk to her?" Leigh hated faking ignorance, but she had little choice.

"No. I turned around and walked out. I thought she was gone for good. Now she's back, like nothing ever happened."

"And that bothers you?"

"Maybe it shouldn't. But there was a baby, Leigh. My baby. She said she was going to get rid of it. I don't know if she meant to give it away or just get an abortion. But it's gone, and I guess I'll never know what became of it." He shook his dark head. "There's no way I'd ask her. I'm the last person on earth she'd talk to. But I can't seem to get past it. I keep wondering if it was a boy or a girl, and how it would have looked."

"Oh, Kevin." Leigh ached to tell him about Mikey— how sweet he was, how bright and how loved. But knowing the truth would turn her brother's whole life upside down.

How long could she keep it from him? Her secret was like a ticking bomb that threatened to blow up at any moment, wounding all the people she held dear.

"All you can do is move on," she said. "You have a good life ahead of you. Make the most of it." Platitudes, she thought; empty words to mask the biggest secret she'd ever kept.

Maybe she should quit her nanny job and leave town— do it before Wyatt, Kevin or Chloe learned the truth. It would tear her apart to leave Mikey, but better now than later, under bad circumstances.

The more she thought about quitting, the more sense the idea made. Mikey was off to a good start with people who'd grown to love him. Chloe, too, would be all right, although Leigh had grown fond of the spunky teen and would miss her.

As for Wyatt...

She had to face it—the reality of never seeing him again. She'd built a world of fantasies around the man— loving him and being loved, sharing his bed, sharing his life. But even without her secret, none of those fantasies had stood a chance of coming true. And with the secret, sooner or later Wyatt was bound to find out how she'd played him. He would be hurt and angry. In all likelihood he would never forgive her.

Better to leave now, with her secret intact. Learning the truth after she was gone would, at least, lessen the blow to his pride.

By the next afternoon, with the Mercedes pulling out of the driveway, Leigh had made up her mind. According to the terms of her contract she was still on probation. That meant she could leave without notice. She would spend a couple of days putting things in order. Then she would walk out the door and never look back.

Leaving wouldn't be easy. But Chloe was competent with Mikey by now, and Dora was available if needed. They would manage fine until Wyatt could hire a new nanny.

Their lives would go on. So would hers. But she couldn't remain in Dutchman's Creek. A girlfriend in Denver had invited her to visit. That would give her a chance to do some job hunting. There had to be something for an unemployed journalist, even if it turned out to be waiting tables.

She was doing the right thing, she told herself. She would make this work for all concerned. She had to.

By the time she pulled up to the house it was getting dark. Powdery snowflakes, fine as sand, drifted down from the twilight sky. Wyatt was waiting on the front porch, lamplight silvering his thick hair. Dressed in jeans and a bulky ski sweater, he looked so strong and handsome that he almost stopped her heart.

Hurrying down the stone steps, he opened the car door for her, then took the keys and strode around to retrieve her suitcase from the back.

"Come in and get warm," he said. "I'll put the car away later. I was getting worried about you."

"Traffic was bad. A fender bender at the turnoff." Leigh stomped the light snow off her boots. As he opened the door, the smell of warm chili and cheese biscuits enfolded her like a welcome.

Chloe was waiting in the entry with a fussing Mikey in her arms. As Leigh shed her jacket, the girl thrust the baby toward her. "Thank goodness you're back, Leigh. Mikey's been a little stinker. I think he missed you."

As Leigh gathered him close, Mikey stopped crying and nestled against her shoulder. Leigh kissed the top of his downy head, her heart flooding with love. She'd felt so resolute in the car. But leaving these people was going to be the hardest thing she'd ever done.

"Are you hungry, Leigh?" Wyatt asked. "We kept some supper warm for you."

"Famished. I just hope Mikey will let me eat."

"I'll hold him." Wyatt took his grandson and made a cradle with his arms. Mikey fussed a moment before he found a fist to suck on.

The table had been cleared except for one place setting. While Leigh dished up chili and biscuits, Wyatt took a seat on the opposite side. "Don't you have schoolwork, Chloe?" he asked.

She pulled a face at him and disappeared in the direction of her room. "She's a smart girl," he said, giving Leigh a look that triggered a flutter in the pit of her stomach. She took her place at the table, deliberately avoiding eye contact with his penetrating gaze. What was he about to say to her? Had he already discovered what she was hiding?

Maybe she should quit now and spare herself the humiliation of being fired.

"I've been waiting to talk to you. But now that you're here, I feel like a schoolboy asking a girl to his first prom. I'd like to take you out on a Friday night date, Leigh."

At that, she finally looked up. "A date?"

"A real one. Every year I host a charity reception at the lodge to celebrate the opening of the winter season. We could spend an hour there, then sneak off and have a nice, private dinner at the hotel."

"What about…?" She nodded in the direction of Chloe's room.

"She's going to a slumber party at her friend's house. I've arranged for Dora to watch Mikey. So what do you say?"

Leigh fixed her gaze on the woven place mat. She understood what his invitation implied. They would have time alone, all the time they needed.

Did she want it to happen? But why ask? She'd wanted Wyatt Richardson from the first day they'd met. And ever since he'd made love to her, she'd burned to do it again.

Leigh knew it wouldn't be forever. Wyatt wasn't a forever kind of man. He was too driven, too focused on building his empire. In any case, she planned on leaving before he learned her secret. So why not? Why shouldn't Cinderella enjoy a night at the ball with Prince Charming before the clock struck twelve?

"Leigh?"

She looked up. In his lake-blue eyes she caught a glint of vulnerability. That alone gave her courage. Forcing a mischievous smile, she replied with a question.

"How could a girl refuse a man with a baby in his arms?"

* * *

Leigh had nothing to wear to a fancy-dress reception. But the resort's trendy boutiques stocked everything from ski clothes to formal wear. A delighted Chloe organized a Thursday shopping expedition. With Mikey bundled into his carrier, they trudged the heated boardwalks, looking, commenting, trying and comparing. Wyatt had told Leigh to charge her purchase to the resort. But she'd insisted on paying out of her own pocket. When she finally found the perfect dress, she was grateful for the generous salary that allowed her to splurge.

The one-shouldered cocktail-length gown was a dark, subtly iridescent emerald-green. On the hanger it looked like nothing more than a limp tube of fabric. But when Leigh stepped out of the fitting room the salesgirl gasped and Chloe cheered.

Their search was over. Almost. Leigh had planned to make do with her black pumps, but Chloe insisted on treating her to a spectacular pair of lattice-cut, high-heeled gold boots. They were the sort of footwear Leigh would never have picked for herself, but they added an elegantly funky touch to the simple gown.

It hadn't escaped Leigh's notice that she and Chloe wore the same shoe size. When the evening was over she would give the expensive boots to Wyatt's daughter—something Chloe may have had in mind all along.

After downing mugs of hot chocolate with whipped cream, they packed Mikey and their purchases into the Mercedes. It had been a good afternoon. Feeling relaxed and pleasantly tired, Leigh drove the canyon road. Her mind had begun to wander when Chloe's question jerked her back to the present.

"Leigh, are you in love with my father?"

With effort, Leigh found her voice. "Why do you ask?"

"I can tell he likes you a lot. I was just wondering if you feel the same about him. Do you?"

"Do I like him? Yes, very much."

"But do you love him?"

This was getting tough. "I could," Leigh said, "if I thought things might work out for us. But I'm afraid that's not going to happen."

"Why not, if you like each other so much?"

Leigh sighed. "I want a family. That's something your father doesn't seem to have time for. Besides, he's had a lot of beautiful girlfriends. You said so yourself. Why should he settle for me?"

"Because you're smart. Because you're clearly not after his money. And because you get along with Mikey and me." Chloe's hands clasped on her knees. "Why don't you stay? You and Daddy could even get married."

Leigh's stomach had tightened into a knot. Why was it becoming so painful to leave these people? "It's not that simple, Chloe," she said. "Maybe your father likes me, but I can't imagine he loves me."

"How do you know?"

"How does anybody know? By the things people say— by the way they treat you."

Chloe slumped a little. "I don't think anybody's ever loved me. For sure not my mother. And maybe not my dad, either."

"Chloe, I know your father loves you."

"Then why hasn't he ever spent time with me? All he's ever done is work—and buy me stuff!"

Leigh turned onto the narrow road that led up to the house. "Maybe that's his way of showing love—being a good provider."

"Well, it sucks!"

"What if it's the only way he knows?"

"Still sucks."

"Well, Mikey loves you. You're his mother."

She brightened. "Yes, he does! Don't you, Mikey?" She reached back over the top of the car seat and ruffled her baby's hair. "You're my own little baby. And I'm going to love you forever. I'll never kick you out like my mother kicked me out!"

As the car turned up the drive, Leigh reached over and patted the girl's arm. "You're just beginning to learn about love, Chloe. All of us—your father, me, even your mother—we're all still learning."

Had she said the right thing? Leigh pulled up to the house and saw Wyatt waiting on the porch. He'd been shoveling snow, and his cheeks were ruddy with cold. Leigh's heart softened at the sight of him. Why was love such a confusing emotion? What if she didn't know any more about it than Chloe did?

On Friday the afternoon sun was warm enough to melt the snow on the plowed roads. Late in the day, Chloe's friend Amy showed up in a red convertible. Blowing a kiss to Mikey, Chloe grabbed her overnight bag and skipped out the door like a newly freed prisoner. Wyatt scowled as he watched the car flash around the first curve. "Kids," he muttered to himself. "They drive like they think they're immortal."

Tearing his gaze away from the road, he carried Mikey back inside. He'd offered to tend the baby while Leigh showered and washed her hair. It pleased him that she and Chloe had gone shopping together. They'd kept her dress a secret, but Leigh would look ravishing in a gunnysack. He looked forward to walking into the ballroom with her on his arm.

"What do you think, big guy?" he asked Mikey. "Will this old man be around when you learn to drive a car?"

Mikey cooed and blew a bubble. He was growing so fast, changing day by day. Before long he'd be sitting up and crawling, then walking and talking. Every day brought its own small miracles. How many more of those days would he get to share? Wyatt wondered. Would Chloe stay here and raise her son, or would she spread her wings and take him far away? She'd most likely marry in a few years. What would become of Mikey then? Time passed so fast.

Speaking of time… He glanced at the clock. He was anxious to get Leigh where he could have her to himself. From her bathroom upstairs the sound of running water stirred a fantasy. He imagined himself stripped down, stepping into the spacious shower with her and running his soaped hands over the delicious curves of her body—her breasts, her hips, her thighs…maybe before the night was over even better things would happen.

Mikey sneezed. Looking down at his grandson, Wyatt chuckled. "What would you say if you knew what your old man was thinking? Would you be shocked?"

The eyes gazing up at him were as pure as the sky. The band of love around Wyatt's heart jerked tight—tight enough to hurt.

The reception was scheduled to start at seven-thirty with cocktails, a lavish buffet and a silent charity auction to raise funds for scholarships for needy students. Wyatt's staff was handling the arrangements, but he needed to be there on time to greet the guests.

Dora arrived at the house a few minutes early. She fussed over Mikey and kidded Wyatt about his tuxedo. "Don't you look gorgeous!" she exclaimed. "If I was ten years younger I'd have a hard time keeping my hands off you. Where's Leigh?"

"She'll be down in a minute. You know enough about this place to make yourself at home. There's plenty to eat in the kitchen, and Leigh says you can stretch out on her bed after Mikey goes down for the night."

"I take it you might be late." Wyatt's longtime head of Housekeeping was no fool.

"We'll see. In any case, I'll have my cell phone with me. If you have concerns about Mikey or anything else, don't hesitate to call."

"I've got you on speed dial." Dora lifted Mikey out of his carrier and kissed his plump cheek. "Come on, Mr. Mikey. You and I are gonna party tonight!"

Wyatt glanced up at the sound of clicking heels overhead. Seconds later Leigh appeared at the top of the stairs. His heart stalled at the sight of her.

The first thing he noticed was the dress. Modest but incredibly sexy, it clung to every curve, exposing one creamy shoulder, defining her slim waist and skimming the tops of her knees. Its glowing green color brought out the gold flecks in her eyes. Her hair was twisted loosely at the crown of her head, with stray tendrils framing her glowing face. Gold hoops, the only jewelry she wore, dangled from her earlobes.

But the pièce de résistance was the gold boots. So outrageous that only Chloe could have chosen them, they clung to Leigh's magnificent legs, their open-cut design showing glimpses of porcelain skin beneath.

Teetering slightly on five-inch stilettos, Leigh clung to the banister as she negotiated each step. Wyatt sprinted up the stairs to take her arm. Only then did he notice that her free hand clasped her black pumps. "Just in case my feet don't last," she muttered. "We can leave them in the car."

He laughed. "You'll be fine. Just hang on to me. You look stunning, by the way."

"Thanks. Chloe was a lot of help. And you clean up nicely yourself."

Wyatt steadied her until they reached the bottom landing. He found himself wishing they could just skip the reception and go straight to the penthouse. He wanted this woman all to himself.

Finding her woolen coat in the closet, he held it while she slipped her arms into the sleeves. "I'd like to wrap you in ermine," he murmured, pulling it around her.

She laughed. "That would be a waste. I don't wear little furry animals."

"That doesn't surprise me. You're a very gentle person, Leigh." He put on his own coat and led her outside where the Mercedes was parked next to Dora's sedan. With Leigh on his arm, he felt a foot taller and ten years younger. He could hardly wait to show her off.

Pulse humming with anticipation, he helped her into the car. Her fragrance teased his nostrils as he started the engine. He inhaled, filling his senses. Tonight was going to be good, he told himself. Not just good. If he had his way it would be perfect.

Ten

Willing herself to not appear nervous, Leigh waited for Wyatt to check their coats. The guests were just beginning to arrive. She recognized a few of them from her work at the newspaper. Most were strangers. But all of them looked rich. Heaven help her, they even *smelled* rich.

Most of the women were older and more conservatively dressed than Leigh. Clad in designer gowns, their ears, hands and throats sparkling with real jewels, they made her feel like some sort of disco queen. Why had she let Chloe help choose her outfit—especially those ridiculous boots?

Wyatt joined her, his hand resting beneath her elbow. "You look like a goddess," he whispered, bending his head to her ear. "Every man in the room is going to be jealous of me."

And the women? They could be pecking her apart like clucking hens—probably thinking she was some gold-digging tart after Wyatt's money.

But never mind. She was with the most important man

here, and she wasn't an idiot. She knew how to be gracious and personable, and she would do her best.

"Hang on to me," she whispered as Wyatt walked her across the freshly waxed floor. "I don't want to fall down—or embarrass you in any other way."

"You'll do fine." He chuckled and squeezed her arm. "Just relax and be your beautiful self."

The rustic ballroom was decorated for the holidays with garlands of evergreen that filled the room with fragrance. Bows of plaid satin, trimmed with pine cones and brass sleigh bells, anchored the greenery in place. Chandeliers glittered overhead. Behind a wrought iron screen, logs blazed in the huge stone fireplace.

Soon Wyatt was mingling with his guests, introducing her as "Ms. Leigh Foster." Teetering on her five-inch heels, Leigh greeted each one with a smile and what she hoped was a nice personal comment. Some of the men practically bowed over her hand. The more common reaction from the women was a frosty glare, but Leigh quickly got used to that. She was actually beginning to have a good time.

At the far end of the room was a bar and a long, lavishly set buffet table. Liveried waiters, balancing trays of drinks and hors d'oeuvres, circulated among the guests. On a dais in one corner, a jazz trio played classic Gershwin. The female singer who stepped up to the microphone was one of Leigh's mother's favorites. Her warm, husky voice wafted through the crowd. Leigh sighed. How her mother would have loved to share this evening.

By now the ballroom was filling up. Some of the new arrivals were younger women in short, glittering dresses and high platform shoes. Their presence made Leigh feel less of a sore thumb. She even caught a few admiring glances at her boots. She was going to be all right.

"Can I get you something, Leigh?" Wyatt asked.

"You mentioned dinner. If we're still on for that, I can wait. I don't want to spoil my appetite." And, truth be told, she didn't want to lose her balance and drop her food.

"Some champagne, maybe?"

She shook her head. "I'm fine. Alcohol makes me tipsy." And being tipsy, Leigh reminded herself, was the last thing she needed tonight.

The other guests seemed to have no such concerns. Most of them were drinking, some heavily, but everyone seemed to be in a jolly mood. Hopefully they'd be writing generous checks for charity.

"How long are we planning to stay?" she whispered to Wyatt.

"Not much longer." His sexy, secret smile sent a shimmer all the way to her toes. "I've got a few more people to greet. After that we can sneak out early. Are you getting tired?"

She returned his smile. "I'm fine. Take your— *Oh!*" She staggered sideways as a linebacker-sized man bumped her shoulder on his way to the bar. Wyatt's quick reflexes saved her from a fall, but as he pulled her upright, she felt a stabbing sensation in her left ankle. She bit back a cry.

"Are you all right?" His eyes probed her face. "No, you aren't. I can tell."

"I'll be fine," Leigh said. "Just gave my ankle a little twist. We don't need to leave." As if to prove her words, she took a step on her injured leg. The pain made her gasp.

"We are leaving. Now." In one motion he swept her up in his arms and strode to the passageway that connected the lodge and the hotel. Leigh curled against his chest, feeling every eye in the ballroom on them.

"Is this what you call sneaking out?" she asked. "We're going to be the talk of the party."

"Who cares?" As they approached the hotel lobby, he

took a turn toward a hidden elevator, punching a code on the panel next to the door. The door slid open and closed behind them without a sound. Inside, the elevator was paneled in aromatic cedar wood and floored with a rich Persian carpet. There were no floor stops. It carried them straight up, like a rocket rising into space.

"Wyatt, where is this taking us?" Leigh whispered in hushed wonder.

"You'll see." His laugh tickled her ear. "How's your ankle?"

"Hard to tell. It just feels numb."

"I'll check it when we stop. If it looks like anything serious, the resort keeps a paramedic on call. Not quite what I'd planned, I'll confess."

"What had you planned? Tell me the truth."

"The perfect evening in the perfect place."

"With the very imperfect Miss Foster? You had to know something would go wrong."

"Not imperfect in my book. I've waited a long time for this night, Leigh." His lips brushed her hair. "And I'm not giving up on it yet."

The elevator had come to a stop. The door glided open to reveal a suite so elegant that Leigh was struck speechless. Three of the walls were floor-to-ceiling glass, the lights kept low to reveal a vast panorama of the stars, the moon and the snow-crested peaks above the resort. Outside the far wall was a terrace, its landscape of shrubs and trees festooned with a hundred thousand tiny white lights. Tendrils of steam rose from a heated pool, glowing like a flawless turquoise among the rocks.

What she could see of the shadowed parlor area appeared to be furnished with massive dark chairs and a long couch arranged on a white rug. Flames in a copper fire pit with filigreed sides lent warmth and soft, golden light.

Wyatt lowered her into one cushiony chair. Switching on a table lamp, he knelt at her feet and unzipped the back of her boot. Leigh hadn't bothered with panty hose tonight. His touch sent delicious tingles up her bare leg.

Very gently he freed her foot. "I don't see any swelling. How does this feel?" He rotated the foot slightly.

She winced. "I can feel it. But it's not too bad."

"I'd say it's nothing to worry about. Maybe a mild sprain. Give it some rest and you should be fine."

"I'm sorry to have been such a baby."

"You weren't a baby." He unzipped her other boot and slipped it off her foot. "But you did give me a good excuse to get you out of that party."

Leigh's breath caught as his hand slid up her leg to her thigh. She'd been aching to be touched by him, but she hadn't counted on the deep well of emotion he'd opened up. Wyatt's touch wasn't enough. She wanted his love. But what was she thinking? She might as well want the moon.

Rising on his knees he leaned into her, his mouth capturing hers in a deep, intimate kiss. Letting go of her doubts, she let her response flow—her lips parting, her tongue mingling with his, her unbridled fingers furrowing his hair. She'd allow herself this one night with him. She would make every second count. Then tomorrow she would quit her job and walk away.

To stay longer would only break hearts—hers and others'.

His hand moved higher, his touch sure and confident. She opened to him, her head spinning as he found her lacy panties and pushed the crotch aside. She was already wet enough for his fingers to glide over her moisture-slicked folds. She moaned as he found their center, pressing against his hand to heighten the exquisite feeling. "I've wanted you, Leigh," he muttered. "Wanted you so damned much I could hardly stand it...."

Stroking her with his thumb, he slid a finger inside her. Already aroused, she came fast, exploding to a climax against his hand. She gave a little cry, her body shuddering.

As the rapture ebbed, her head fell against his shoulder.

He chuckled in her ear. "More to come. Meanwhile, I believe I promised you dinner."

Rising, he clicked what looked like a remote control. The elevator door slid open to reveal a white-draped cart holding champagne in a bucket of ice, several covered dishes and a bouquet of two dozen red roses in a crystal vase. "Just in time, I see." Wyatt rinsed his hands and wheeled the cart into the room. There was no waiter. Evidently he'd requested that the cart be sent up alone.

Glancing around, Leigh noticed a dining alcove with the table set for two. Whisking the food and flowers onto the table, Wyatt lit a pair of candles, popped the champagne cork and filled two crystal flutes with the sparkling liquid. "Back in the day, I earned my ski passes at Vail by working as a waiter," he said, helping Leigh to her chair. "Still haven't lost my touch."

"You've come a long way," Leigh said.

"Yes, I have. And I like where I am. Especially tonight." He took his seat. His hand moved across the tablecloth to rest on hers. "You take my breath away, Leigh. You have from the moment you walked into that interview."

"I still can't believe you hired me. You must've been desperate."

"I was. But I know a good thing when I see it. You and Mikey have turned my solitary world upside down. And, believe it or not, I've come to like it." Raising his champagne flute, he held it toward her. "To one lovely night."

What was he trying to do to her? Had he guessed that

she was going to quit? Was he twisting the blade, making everything more painful?

"One lovely night." She repeated the toast, touched her glass to his and drained it.

Dinner was delicious—Rock Cornish game hens with mushroom stuffing, cooked in wine sauce and served on a bed of fresh kale from the resort's organic greenhouse. For dessert there were rum-flavored miniature cream puffs garnished with slivers of chocolate—decadent but not too filling.

Keeping the champagne and the two crystal flutes, Wyatt whisked the dishes back onto the cart, rolled it into the elevator and clicked the remote. As the doors closed, his gaze wandered to the blue pool on the terrace. "A nice warm soak might be good for your ankle," he said.

"It might. But it's cold outside."

"No problem." He clicked another button on the remote. Heat lamps surrounding the pool began to glow. "There's a robe for you on the back of the bathroom door."

"I don't suppose there's a bathing suit. I didn't bring one."

He grinned impishly. "Neither did I."

The robe was a cloud of plush white terry cloth. It felt heavenly against Leigh's bare skin as she wrapped it around her body and tied the sash. There were cushiony white spa slippers, as well. Limping a little she made her way back to the parlor. The glass door to the terrace slid open at her approach. More tricks with the remote, she surmised.

Wyatt was already in the pool, his own robe draped over a chair. Even blurred by the bubbling water jets, the lights below the surface left little to the imagination. "If you're nervous, I can close my eyes," he teased.

"I'll take that as a challenge." Locking her gaze with

his, she stepped out of her slippers and untied the sash of her robe. As the garment fell open, she slipped it off her arms and laid it on a bench outside the circle of heat lamps. A chilly breeze struck her body.

"You've got goose bumps," Wyatt said. "Come on in and get warm."

Leigh needed no more urging. Finding the stone steps she lowered herself into the pool and sank in up to her shoulders. The heated water was lightly scented with rosemary. "This feels...marvelous," she breathed.

"Told you." Wyatt was chest deep on the opposite side of the bed-sized pool. In the glow of the heat lamps he looked tanned, fit and stunningly virile.

"Come here, Leigh." His husky voice was almost a growl. As she moved toward him through the bubbling water he reached out, caught her arm and pulled her against him. Naked, it was obvious that he still had the body of a champion athlete—solid muscle, strong and hard.

"I take it we aren't here for a deep, serious talk," she murmured as his arms tightened around her.

"Uh-uh." His kiss was long and deep and sensual. Their legs tangled under the water. She felt his arousal jutting like a rock against her belly. Reaching down, she clasped him. His size dwarfed her hand. As her fingers tightened, he groaned. "Watch it, lady, if you want to save the best for last."

"Are we going to stay here?"

"Lovemaking underwater is overrated. I have a better place in mind. Meanwhile just lie back and relax."

Turning her back to him, he cupped his hands beneath her breasts, and eased her head into the hollow of his shoulder. Her feet floated outward in the bubbling water. "Lovely," she whispered.

"So are you." His hands fondled her breasts, lightly

thumbing the nipples. A slow, sweet ache tightened between her legs. "When you're nice and warm let me know and we'll get out," he said.

"I may go to sleep right here."

"That's fine as long as you let me wake you up."

She closed her eyes, luxuriating in the bubbles and the caressing strokes of his strong but gentle hands. A man who put a woman's pleasure before his own was her kind of man. Too bad this one wasn't for keeps.

She could feel her body respond to him. Heat shimmered from her breasts into her limbs and down into her pulsing core. She wanted him in every way a woman could want a man. And she couldn't stand to wait any longer.

Turning in the water she seized his head and kissed him, not timidly but with all the stops out. He seized her with a rough laugh, no longer gentle as he lifted her out of the water and mounted the steps. Setting her down, he flung her robe around her and reached for his own. The thick fabric soaked up the moisture.

Without a word he scooped her into his arms again and strode inside. The bedroom was dark. She glimpsed a vast turned-down bed before he slipped off her robe and lowered her onto the silk sheets. She sank into the featherbed, cradled by its sumptuous warmth, while he paused to add protection. As he leaned over the bed her arms reached up, pulling him down to her. He laughed. "Eager little thing, aren't you?" he teased. "Just hold on."

He began kissing her—her eyelids, her lips, her throat. She whimpered as his skilled mouth worked downward to her breasts, flicking and suckling the nipples until her body burned. Still he gave her no mercy, no blessed release. His kisses skimmed her belly, blazing a trail to her hot, moist center, parting the petal-like folds with a flick of his tongue. She came in a flash, whimpering as she arched against him. But it wasn't enough. "Wyatt…now…" she pleaded.

Pushing forward, he entered her in a single gliding thrust.

As his hard-swollen sex filled the length of her, she felt herself tighten around him. His slightest movement set off fire bursts that rippled through her body. She moved with him, knowing he was lost in her now, and lost in the wild, primal urge that drove their bodies in a frenzy of need. Her head fell back. Indescribable sensations coursed through her veins. She gave a little cry as, with one hard final thrust, he shuddered like a stallion and slumped over her…laughing.

Heaven help her, she could get used to this.

They made love again, then again, until they lay in each other's arms, utterly exhausted. Cradled against him, Leigh inhaled the manly aroma of his damp skin. She loved the smell of him, the feel of him, the husky timbre of his voice. She couldn't ask for more than to spend every night of her life with this man.

But it wasn't going to happen. Wyatt only wanted a fling, and if she stayed until he learned the truth, he wouldn't even want that. Once he uncovered what she'd kept from him, he would hate her—and his vengeance on her brother could destroy Kevin's life.

Tomorrow, come what may, she would resign from her job and resolve to never see him—or Mikey—again.

Opening one eye, she glanced at the bedside clock. It was 1:15 a.m. They hadn't planned to stay the night. Before long it would be time to get home to Mikey so Dora could leave. But the bed was so soft and warm, Wyatt's nearness so sweet. She would rest a few more minutes. Then, if Wyatt hadn't stirred, she would wake him up to leave.

Closing her eyes, she drifted off. The next thing she

heard was the ringing of Wyatt's cell phone on the night-stand.

The sound startled her awake. Glancing at the clock again she saw that it was after two o'clock. Wyatt muttered groggily, sat up and reached for the phone.

"Hello?…Yes, what is it, Dora?"

Leigh was suddenly wide-awake. As the conversation continued she reached for her clothes and began getting dressed.

"He's *what?*…How high?…Yes, that's a good idea. We'll meet you there." He hung up the phone and turned to Leigh with a somber expression.

"What is it?" She stared at him, cold fear closing around her heart.

"It's Mikey." His voice was flat. "He's running a fever, seems to have a lot of congestion. Dora's taking him to the hospital. We'll meet her there. She thinks he might have pneumonia."

Eleven

A valet was waiting at the hotel entrance with the Mercedes and their coats. Leigh, who'd chosen to wear the spa slippers downstairs and carry her gold boots, was grateful she'd thought to leave her pumps in the car. But her feet were the least of her worries now. She imagined her precious baby desperately sick and struggling to breathe. What if Dora didn't make it to the hospital in time?

Wyatt drove as fast as the wheels could take the curves, his mouth set in a grim line. Beside him, Leigh kept a lookout for deer. "What do you know about pneumonia?" she asked him.

"Next to nothing. But I trust Dora's judgment. She was concerned enough to take Mikey right to the hospital." He handed her his cell phone. "We'd better let Chloe know. She'll want to be there."

Leigh scrolled down to Chloe's number and speed dialed. She heard the phone ring on the other end. It rang again, then again until Chloe's message voice came on, followed by a beep.

"Chloe, this is Leigh. Mikey's sick. He's on his way to the hospital. Call your dad when you get this."

"She's not answering?" Wyatt shot her an anxious look as she ended the call.

Leigh shook her head. "I'll try again in a few minutes. She might be asleep with the phone turned off."

"Asleep? This early? At a slumber party? That would be a first." Wyatt was trying to make light of things, but Leigh could tell he was worried. Not only about his grandson but about his daughter.

Even at high speed, with no traffic on the road, the ride down the canyon seemed to take forever. Leigh tried to call Chloe again, then again. There was no answer.

"What about the girl having the party?" she asked Wyatt. "Do you know where she lives?"

"No, but I called her mother before I agreed to let Chloe go. I may have put the number in my wallet. I'll look when we get to the hospital."

They pulled onto the main road and sped through the sleeping town. Leigh's pulse quickened when she spotted Dora's car in the hospital parking lot. At least she'd made it here with Mikey.

Leaving Wyatt to park the Mercedes, she leaped out and raced into the emergency entrance. She found Dora in the waiting room. The two women embraced. "They took him in a few minutes ago," Dora said. "We can go back once they've got him stabilized."

"Will he be all right?"

"Let's hope so. One of my babies had pneumonia so I know the signs. He's one sick little boy."

Wyatt rushed in through the double doors. Dora updated him on Mikey's condition.

"You said you were going to look for that phone number," Leigh reminded him.

He thumbed through his wallet and came up with a scrap of paper. "This is it. Let's hope they can rouse Chloe."

He'd found his cell phone and was about to dial the number when a nurse came into the waiting room. "We've got your baby on oxygen and an IV. You can go back and be with him if you'd like." She glanced at Leigh. "Are you his mother?"

"No, I'm—"

"She might as well be," Dora interrupted. "Just go, Leigh."

The nurse asked no more questions. Leaving Dora in the waiting area, Leigh and Wyatt followed her back along a hallway to a small room. Mikey lay in an incubator wearing nothing but a disposable diaper. An IV tube was attached by a needle to one tiny foot. His eyes were closed, his skin slightly blue. He looked so small and pathetic that Leigh wanted to weep. Her cold hand crept into Wyatt's.

Wyatt tightened his fingers around hers, taking and giving comfort. Looking down at his helpless little grandson, he felt a surge of love so powerful that it seemed to crush his heart. This little boy, neither expected nor wanted at first, had become the most precious thing on earth. Wyatt could no longer imagine life without him.

A bespectacled young man—presumably the doctor—stood beside the table making notes on a clipboard. "We've got your son on an antibiotic and we've suctioned him as best we can," he said. "I've seen worse cases pull through, and I'd say his chances are good. But the next few hours will be critical."

Your son. The doctor had assumed he and Leigh were Mikey's parents.

"Can I stay here with him?" Leigh asked.

"Sure." He nodded toward a chair in the corner. "There's coffee at the nurses' station. Restroom's across the hall."

Her hand slipped out of his. "You need to find Chloe. I'll call you if anything changes."

He nodded, taking a few more seconds to look down at Mikey. "Hang in there, big guy," he whispered. Then he tore himself away and walked back to the waiting room.

Dora was thumbing restlessly through a magazine. She rose as she saw him. "Thanks for getting Mikey here so fast," he told her. "He's not out of the woods yet, but the doctor seems optimistic."

"Thank goodness!"

"Leigh's going to stay with him. You're welcome to go home and get some rest."

She shook her head. "I won't rest till I know Mikey's all right. Where's Chloe?"

"That's what I'm trying to find out." Wyatt found his cell phone again and punched in the number his daughter had given him earlier. After several rings, a woman's sleepy voice answered.

"Sorry to wake you, Mrs. Winslow. This is Wyatt Richardson. I need to speak with Chloe. It's an emergency."

There was a pause on the other end of the line. "Chloe isn't here."

"What?"

"She was here for a while. But around ten she said she was feeling sick. Amy drove her home. Isn't she there?"

Wyatt felt his nerves clench. "Did Amy come back?"

"No. I assumed she'd stayed with Chloe or gone home."

Wyatt exhaled, forcing himself to speak calmly. "It's urgent that I find her. I'll need to speak to the other girls. One of them might know where she's gone. Do you mind if I come to your house?"

There was a beat of hesitation. "Of course not. I'll make some coffee."

"That won't be necessary." Wyatt got the address, jotted it down and ended the call.

Dora gazed at him in dismay, clearly having grasped what had happened from overhearing his side of the call. "That little pill ought to be locked up till she's twenty-one! I'll stay out here in case she shows."

"Thanks." Wyatt was out the door, racing to his car. He'd hoped motherhood was making Chloe more responsible. But he should have known better.

He recognized the neighborhood. The Winslow home wasn't far from the house he'd bought for Tina. The porch light was on, as was a lamp in the front room. Evidently the girls had been alerted that he was coming.

Mrs. Winslow, a petite blonde of Tina's vintage, answered the front door. She was dressed in a black silk robe and he noticed she'd put on fresh makeup. If there was a Mr. Winslow, he was nowhere to be seen. Not that it mattered.

After listening to his brief apology, she ushered him into the living room. Five girls in pajamas sat huddled on the sectional sofa looking like suspects in a police lineup.

Wyatt frowned at them. "Let's make this fast. Chloe's baby is in the hospital, very sick, and I need to find her. If any one of you can tell me where she's gone I'll be grateful—and so will she."

In the silence, the girls looked at each other. Finally one of them raised her hand. "Chloe and Amy went to Jimmy McFarland's house. His folks are out of town for the weekend so he's having a party. They said we'd be in big trouble if we told."

Wyatt exhaled. "You did the right thing. Now I need Jimmy's address."

The girls buzzed among themselves. Mrs. Winslow handed them a pen and notebook. One of them wrote down some directions. "It's a big house like the ones in England," she said. "You can't miss it."

Thanking the girls and Mrs. Winslow, who told him her name was Eve and that he could call her anytime, Wyatt returned to his car. It took him fifteen minutes to find the street.

No, he surmised as he turned the corner, there was no missing the oversized, rambling Tudor. Not with three flashing police cars pulled up in front.

His pulse quickened, pumping a rush of adrenaline. He could deal with Chloe's misbehavior later. Right now all that mattered was finding her and getting her safely to the hospital.

Passing in front of the house he noticed Amy's red convertible in the drive. Wyatt made a U-turn at the next corner and parked the Mercedes down the block on the opposite side of the street. Climbing out, he kept to the shadows as he approached the house.

The police officers were still in their cars, talking on their radios. Wyatt saw a half-dozen boys sneak around the side of the garage and disappear up the street at a dead run. If they'd come out a back door it should still be unlocked.

Slipping back the way the boys had come, Wyatt emerged on the patio. The outdoor pool had been drained and covered for the winter. There was nobody outside. But he found one of the French doors ajar. Mindful of the risk, he stepped inside. The air reeked with the smell of weed. If the police caught him here he'd have some tall explaining to do. But he had to find his daughter.

Anger roiled in the back of his mind. For the stunt she'd pulled, Chloe deserved to be arrested and maybe spend a night in jail. The experience might even teach her a lesson. But with her baby in the hospital, he knew he couldn't let that happen.

With the police outside, he'd wondered why there weren't more people fleeing the house. As he stepped into the living room he saw the reason. Teenagers were sprawled on the floor and draped over the furniture, most of them too drunk or too stoned to get up and leave. Heartsick, he scanned the dimly lit room for Chloe. He didn't see her.

A boy came out of the kitchen. At least this one was on his feet. He stared at Wyatt with glazed eyes.

"Chloe Richardson," Wyatt growled. "Where is she?"

The boy nodded toward a hallway. "Bathroom. Puking her guts out."

Plunging down the hall, Wyatt saw a door ajar and recognized the sounds coming from the other side. Chloe was hunched over the toilet, in the last stages of being violently sick. She looked up at him, her eyes huge in her chalky face.

"Oh, Daddy, I'm sorry!" she whimpered.

"Never mind. We're getting out of here." He pulled her to her feet and grabbed a towel to wipe her damp face. "Mikey's in the hospital. You need to be with your baby."

"Mikey? Oh, no…." She began to cry. Wyatt dragged her half stumbling out the back door as the police came in the front. Moments later they were safely in the car. Wyatt pulled away from the curb and headed back toward the hospital.

Chloe was sobbing. Wyatt pulled into an all-night drive-up and bought her some coffee. It seemed to calm her a little. "What's wrong with Mikey?" she asked.

"Pneumonia. They've got him in an incubator."

"Will he be okay?"

"I hope so. We'll know for sure in a few hours. Leigh's with him. Dora's there, too. But a baby needs his mother."

"I'm not much of a mother, am I, Daddy?"

Wyatt shot her a dark look. "Don't play the sympathy game with me. You messed up big-time, and there *will* be consequences. For starters, don't plan on having your own car anytime soon. And you're grounded, starting now."

"Oh, please, don't do that," she whined. "I'll never drink again. Cross my heart."

Wyatt sighed, feeling old and tired. "Just be still, Chloe. We'll be at the hospital in a few minutes. Try thinking about Mikey for a change, instead of yourself."

She was mercifully silent for the rest of the drive. Wyatt knew he was partly to blame for what she'd done. He'd never been much of a father to the girl, substituting expensive gifts for what she'd really needed—his time and attention. How could she not grow up spoiled and demanding? How could she not act out in ways that would hurt him and herself?

True, part of the fault was Tina's. What kind of mother would choose her younger husband over her daughter and grandchild? But, looking back now, would Wyatt's ex-wife have evolved into a man-chasing cougar if he'd put more effort into their marriage? Tina's need had been to feel desirable and sexy and loved. When he was too busy to fill that need, she'd looked elsewhere.

At the time neither of them had given much thought to their daughter. Now they were paying the price.

Sadly, so was Chloe.

After an hour on oxygen, Mikey's color had improved and his breathing seemed easier. But the nurse had warned Leigh that it might take several days to kill off the bacteria and clear his lungs. "It doesn't take much to trigger these infections," she'd said. "It can be pretty scary. But if there's one thing I've learned, it's that these little guys want to live, and they're tougher than they look."

Leigh remembered those words as she sat next to the incubator, watching Mikey's every breath and silently praying. Except for a brief trip to update Dora in the waiting room, she hadn't left his side. It was as if, as long as she was there, she could will her love to wrap around his tiny body and keep him safe.

The hospital staff had been more than kind. Taking stock of her skimpy dress and bare legs, they'd found her some scrubs to wear. They'd even brought her coffee and a warm blanket for the chilly room. At least she was more comfortable now. But her gaze kept wandering to the clock on the wall. More than an hour had passed since Wyatt left to look for Chloe. Talons of worry clawed at her strained nerves.

Their passionate night in the hotel penthouse seemed like a faraway dream. Right now only Mikey was real. As she watched the rise and fall of his breathing, Leigh realized that the plan to quit her job wasn't going to happen anytime soon. As long as Mikey was sick she would be here for him. The risk of being found out would rise with each day. And her uncertain relationship with Wyatt would only complicate things. But that was a chance she'd have to take.

Where in heaven's name was he? Were he and Chloe all right?

She'd begun to imagine twisted wreckage and ambulance sirens by the time the door opened. Relief washed over her as Wyatt ushered Chloe into the room. They were both safe.

Then she noticed the girl's pale face and wasted expression. Her clothes reeked of vomit, alcohol and pot fumes.

Wyatt kept a hand at her back as she stumbled toward the incubator and stared down at her helpless baby.

"Oh, Mikey," she whispered, tears streaming down her face. "I'm so sorry."

Leigh patted her clammy hand. "The oxygen is helping him breathe. But the antibiotic may take a while to work. You can thank Dora for getting him here right away."

Chloe's face had paled. She clapped a hand to her mouth. "Gonna be sick," she muttered, staggering toward the door.

"The bathroom's across the hall. I'll go with you." Leigh sprang out of her chair to guide the girl in the right direction, leaving Wyatt in the room.

They made it in the nick of time. Leigh supported Chloe over the bowl as she lost whatever was left in her stomach. "I'm so sorry, Leigh," she whimpered over and over. "So sorry."

Leigh helped her wash her face and hands and dry them on a paper towel. "Why don't you rest in the waiting room with Dora till you feel better? I'll get you a warm blanket and some coffee. Mikey isn't going anywhere."

After getting Chloe settled with Dora, Leigh returned to Mikey's room. She found the door ajar and was about to walk in when she heard Wyatt's voice. He was standing next to the incubator, barely speaking above a whisper. She couldn't resist pausing outside to listen.

"Hang in there, big guy, you hear? Your grandpa has lots of plans for you. He wants to teach you to hike and fish and ski and ride a horse. He wants to get you a puppy and take you to ball games, and send you to college so you can become whatever you want to. But first you need to get better so you can grow up…."

His voice broke. Leigh wiped the wetness from her cheek and opened the door.

His glance swung toward her. Her gaze took in his naked face—the shadows of exhaustion and worry, the glint of vulnerability in his eyes. Here was a man who survived by being in control of everything and everyone around him. Tonight life had yanked that control away, leaving him adrift with nowhere to turn.

Without a word she walked toward him and wrapped her arms around his waist. He held her with all his strength, both of them trembling, both of them scared and needing comfort.

Heaven help her, what a disaster.

She loved him.

Twelve

A few days later Mikey was well enough to go home. His lungs were clear, his cheeks pink and his appetite like a little tiger's.

Wyatt bundled his grandson and, with Leigh at his elbow, carried him to the Mercedes. Leigh looked exhausted. During Mikey's illness she'd scarcely left the boy's side, even spending her nights in the hospital room where he'd been transferred from Emergency. Wyatt had ordered a cot for the room and spelled her when she allowed it, but she'd never left for more than an hour or two, taking time only to shower, change and grab a meal. And she was always there at night.

For a salaried nanny she'd shown an extraordinary measure of devotion. Wyatt might have suspected some ulterior motive, but he'd seen the way she looked at his grandson. What he read in those haunting eyes couldn't be mistaken for anything but love.

In the parking lot he opened the front passenger door for Leigh and handed the baby to Chloe, who sat in back with his carrier. "Hi, Mikey," she chirped as she buckled him in. "I've missed you!"

Along with the expected hangover, Chloe had come down with a nasty cold the morning after her escapade. It had given Wyatt an excuse to keep her at home, but it had also forced him to be there with her instead of spending more time at the hospital. Sadly, he could no longer trust his daughter to behave on her own.

Was Chloe a budding alcoholic who needed to be in rehab, or just a wild teen going through a phase? Tina had been a drinker, he recalled. Alcohol had contributed to her infidelity and their divorce. No way would he allow their daughter to go down the same road. Something had to be done, but what?

Inwardly he sighed. There was no getting around it. He would have to talk the situation over with her mother.

What had happened to him? Not that long ago he'd thought he had everything under control. Then Chloe had shown up on his doorstep, followed by Mikey and Leigh. Now his personal world was in chaos.

But the chaos wasn't entirely bad, Wyatt reminded himself. Leigh and Mikey had opened new windows of light and love in his heart. And fate had given him one last chance to get it right with his little girl. So far, on that front, he wasn't doing so well, but he wasn't going to stop trying—with Chloe or with Leigh and Mikey.

He glanced at Leigh, where she sat beside him. She'd given her all to be there for Mikey. Now she was worn-out. When they got home he was going to insist that she go to bed and get some rest. Chloe was well enough to tend Mikey for the rest of the day.

Once Leigh was feeling better he planned to have a serious talk with her. She wasn't just the nanny anymore. She'd become an important part of his life. Whatever happened with Chloe and Mikey, he wanted her to stay with him—and he'd make it clear that sharing his bed would be part of the bargain. He'd never been good at relationships, but he didn't want to lose this wonderful woman—and lose her he would if he didn't have the courage to take a chance.

Chloe might find the arrangement startling at first. But she liked Leigh and she'd get used to the way of things, especially if he let her know what to expect.

His spirits rose as he swung the Mercedes around the steep mountain curves. Downy snowflakes—always welcome—were drifting from the clouds. He switched on the wipers. He'd called his staff to make sure the house would be warm with a hot lunch waiting and someone to serve. It would be a small celebration of sorts, bringing Mikey home.

He could see the house as they came around the last bend. Parked in the driveway, next to the Wolf Ridge van from the hotel, was an unfamiliar white Cadillac with gold trim. Wyatt's instincts prickled. He wasn't expecting company, especially at home and especially today. But the car was empty, which meant his uninvited guest would be waiting inside the house.

Something wasn't right.

He'd planned to let Leigh, Chloe and the baby out at the front door, then park the Mercedes in the garage. Changing his mind, he pulled up to the porch and went in ahead of them.

As soon as he opened the door, Wyatt knew. It was the perfume, the distinctive, imported scent that filled the air like a miasma.

The petite redhead rose from the couch—movie star hair, chiseled porcelain face, spectacular curves—some of which he'd paid for. She smiled. "Hello, Wyatt."

He felt the day caving in on him. "Hello, Tina," he said.

* * *

Chloe had unfastened the car seat. With Mikey still buckled in, she carried it across the porch and through the front door. Bringing up the rear, Leigh almost bumped into the girl when she halted as if she'd hit a wall.

"Mom!" Chloe's voice blended surprise and a note of what might have been anger. Looking past her, Leigh's weary gaze took in the petite, elegant woman in the clinging black pantsuit.

Wyatt's ex-wife was an older version of her daughter, except that where Chloe's pretty features were natural, her mother's appeared to have been refined by the best cosmetic surgeons in the country. She was too sculpted, too perfect to be real.

But that didn't mean she wasn't beautiful. The woman's polished perfection made Leigh all the more aware of the stringy hair she'd washed in a hurry and air-dried on the way back to the hospital, of her bare face, bloodshot eyes and slept-in clothes.

"What are you doing here, Mom?" Chloe's tone was sullen. "Where's Andre?"

"Let's just say that Andre and I had a…parting of the ways." Her voice was low and sexy, like a blues singer's. "As for what I'm doing here, why shouldn't I want to see my only daughter and her darling baby?"

Chloe stood her ground, gripping the handle of the baby carrier. "Mikey's been sick in the hospital. He mustn't be around strangers yet."

"But I'm not a stranger, dear! I'm little Mikey's… *grandma*." She spoke the word as if she'd just bitten into a bad strawberry.

Leigh gulped back a rush of emotion, thinking how Mikey's *other* grandma would love to see him. Life was so unfair.

Wyatt stepped away from the fireplace where he'd been standing, a glint of steel in his eyes. "Chloe, why don't you take Mikey up to the nursery and put him to bed? Your mother can see him later."

Chloe wheeled and headed for the stairs. Her mother turned on her ex-husband. "You can't do this to me, Wyatt! I have every right to see my own grandchild!"

"Later, Tina." Wyatt shook his head. "The boy's getting over pneumonia and shouldn't be exposed to anything you may have picked up traveling. As for your so-called right, you gave that up when you kicked your pregnant daughter out of the house. How much you see of Mikey now won't be up to me. It will be up to his mother."

"We'll see about that." Turning away from him, she seemed to notice Leigh for the first time. "And who's this? If she's your latest girlfriend, you must be getting desperate."

Torn between following Chloe upstairs and giving the woman her due, Leigh hesitated. She was worn to a frazzle and in no mood to take insults. But she had no wish to worsen the situation by jumping into a catfight.

"Please come here, Leigh." Wyatt's voice held a note of subdued ferocity. Head high, Leigh crossed the room to his side. His hand reached out and came to rest on the small of her back.

"Leigh, my former wife needs no introduction," he said. "Tina, this is Leigh Foster, Mikey's wonderful nanny. She was with him in the hospital day and night. I don't know how we'd have managed without her. As for you, if you can't at least be civil, you're welcome to leave."

In the silence that followed, Tina cocked her head like an elegant bird. Her eyes were jade-green, not blue like Chloe's. "Well…" she said. "My sincere apologies, Miss Foster. I should have realized you weren't Wyatt's type."

With effort, Leigh held her tongue. From the kitchen came the rattle of pans and the drifting aroma of roast beef.

"Lunch is waiting," Wyatt said. "Tina, I don't turn visitors away hungry. You're welcome to stay and eat with us."

"I'll go up and tell Chloe," Leigh offered. "Then, if you don't mind, I'll excuse myself for a nap in a real bed." She hoped Wyatt wouldn't try to argue with her. She was hungry, but the last thing she needed was a tension-filled meal with three people whose issues shouldn't concern her.

"I'll keep a plate warm for you," Wyatt said.

"Sleep tight," Tina called as Leigh mounted the stairs and trudged down the hall to her room. At least meeting the woman had helped her understand the dynamics of Wyatt's family. Chloe might be impulsive and strong-willed, but compared to her mother she was a sweet little lamb.

What was going to happen now that Tina was separated from her husband and back in her daughter's life? Would she stay in Dutchman's Creek? Would Chloe move back with her mother, taking Mikey with her?

Would they want Leigh to go with the baby, or was her time with Kevin's son about to end? Right now she was too tired to reason it out.

After sending Chloe downstairs to eat, she checked on the sleeping Mikey, shed her rumpled clothes, pulled on an old T-shirt and tumbled into bed. The moment her head touched the pillow she fell asleep.

She opened her eyes to a late-day sun casting long shadows across the bed. She felt groggy and disoriented. How long had she slept? Three hours? Four?

Dragging herself out of bed she pattered into the bathroom, where she relieved herself, splashed her face and brushed her teeth. A glance in the mirror showed bloodshot eyes and tangled hair. What now? Should she throw on some clothes? Check on Mikey? Crawl back into bed?

Maybe it was her turn to get sick.

She was still dithering when she heard a polite knock on her door. "Leigh, are you up?" The voice was Wyatt's.

Leigh's T-shirt barely covered her hips. She scrambled back into bed and pulled the covers to her chest before she answered, "Come on in."

Wyatt opened the door. He was carrying a tray with a hot beef sandwich and potato salad on a plate. The food smelled delicious. Her stomach growled. Maybe she wasn't sick after all.

"I heard the water running and thought you might be ready to join the living," he said. "How are you feeling?"

"Better than I look." She fluffed the pillows to support her back. "Where's Mikey?"

"Asleep in Chloe's room. She's on her computer."

"And Tina?"

"Gone for now. Long story. Are you hungry?"

"Starved. And that tray looks good. You're spoiling me, you know."

"I like spoiling you." He set the tray on her lap, unfolded a cloth napkin and tucked it under her chin. "Something tells me you haven't had enough spoiling in your life."

He'd cut the toasted sandwich into neat quarters. Leigh nibbled one. It was succulent and tasty. She took a sip of cold milk. "Careful, I could get used to this," she joked.

"I'd like it if you did." He sat on the foot of the bed, his gaze disturbingly warm. "You've been my rock these past few days. Between Chloe's troubles and the baby, I don't know what I'd have done without you. You've become family, Leigh. I want you to know that. And I want you to stay—with me."

Leigh's appetite fled. Under different conditions, hearing those words from him would have thrilled her. But not now—not when every day she remained here was a betrayal of his trust.

Now would be the time to tell him she was leaving. But he would demand to know why. And then what? How could she go on lying to him? How could she tell him the truth?

"What about your ex-wife?" she asked, groping for a diversion.

"Tina has nothing to do with this. She's rented a house in Denver. At lunch she demanded that Chloe and Mikey move in with her and that you go along to take care of him. Chloe told her, in so many words, to take a hike."

"How can Chloe do that? Tina *is* her mother. And in spite of everything, she must love her daughter."

"She also loves the child support she was getting when Chloe lived with her, especially since her new marriage meant she was no longer entitled to alimony. But we won't go there. I know better than to pass judgment on another parent."

"Who has legal custody of Chloe?"

"We have joint custody. I've always felt that a young girl needed to be with her mother. But now—"

Breaking off, he frowned. "Why are we even talking about this? It's not the reason I'm here."

Leigh waited, bracing herself. She loved this man. But showing her feelings now would be the worst thing she could do.

"I came to tell you that I need you in my life, Leigh. I want more nights like the one we had. I want to spoil you the way I can afford to. And I want to know, that whatever happens with Chloe and Mikey, you and I will be here for each other."

Leigh stared down at the tray on her lap. He hadn't mentioned love. And there'd certainly been no hint of marriage.

But what difference did it make? Even if he'd offered his heart and soul, even if he'd offered her a lifetime, she still couldn't say yes. She couldn't even say maybe. She had to say no and make it stick.

"You're saying you want to promote me from nanny to live-in lover?" The sarcasm would sting. She needed it to. She shook her head. "I've been there. Next time I play that game, I'm playing for keeps—and you're not a 'for keeps' kind of man, Wyatt. You can have any woman you want. After a while you'd get bored with me and start looking around for some excitement."

His expression had turned stony. "I take it that's a no."

"In twenty-two-point, bold caps. *N-O*."

Leigh knew she'd wounded him. Though he hid it well, she'd seen the flicker of hurt in his eyes. It had been all she could do to keep from flinging her arms around him and telling him she'd changed her mind. But no, this had to be done, and now she'd done it.

Wyatt was a proud man. He wouldn't be asking her again. But she needed to make sure.

"Consider this my two-week notice," she said. "I'll stay long enough to make sure Mikey's all right. Meanwhile you can start looking for a new nanny."

As long as he lived, Wyatt swore, he would never understand women. He'd been so sure that Leigh returned his feelings. But when he'd pushed for a long-term relationship, she'd thrown up a wall of resistance and announced she was quitting her job.

Chloe had mentioned earlier that Leigh had been engaged, and that her fiancé had cheated on her. Had the experience soured her for life on the idea of a lasting relationship? Or was she hiding something even deeper?

Wyatt had hoped to talk to her, at least. But she was

making every excuse to avoid him, hanging out in her room with Mikey and only showing up for meals when she knew Chloe would be there. Meanwhile, the days were ticking by like some grim clock. Would she really leave when the two weeks were up? He was determined—make that frantic—to stop her. Leigh Foster was the best thing that had ever happened to him. He couldn't let her walk out of his life without understanding why.

As if his worries about Leigh weren't enough, Tina was haranguing him daily by phone from Denver, threatening legal action if he didn't deliver Chloe and Mikey to her house. Wyatt's lawyer had assured him he had every right to keep his daughter and grandson. But that did little to ease his concerns. His ex-wife was an insecure, frightened woman, alone for the first time in her life. Right or wrong, he still felt some responsibility for her.

Chloe had declared that she would take Mikey and run away before she'd go back to her mother. Since Wyatt had no plans to send her, that wasn't a serious threat. But with Chloe, there were always other issues.

He'd stuck to his guns about punishing her for the drunken party escapade. Both the car and the ski holiday with her friends were on hold, and she was grounded to the house for the next month.

A grounded Chloe was like a caged wildcat. She whined and pouted from morning till night, locking herself in her room with her computer while blasting rap music through the house. If she was going to be miserable, so was everyone else.

The one ray of sunshine in the house was Mikey. He had blossomed into a plump, cooing, cuddling bundle of joy. Wyatt couldn't get enough of him when he was home. And when he was away from home, at least he had his work running the resort.

Today he stood on the side porch of the lodge, watching skiers glide down the powdery runs. It was a beautiful afternoon, the fresh-fallen snow glittering like diamond dust on the slopes. The lifts were full, the restaurants and coffee shops teeming, the lodge filled with the glow of a crackling fire. It cheered him to see what his efforts had built. And he was definitely in need of some cheering.

Last night Chloe had been impossible. It had been the evening of the annual winter carnival at her old school, a party that included a huge outdoor bonfire, hot dogs and s'mores, and a stag dance in the gym. She'd begged to be allowed to go. But Wyatt had stood firm. He knew for a fact that older boys often smuggled liquor into the event. Besides, she was grounded, and that was that.

But Chloe hadn't let up. "I just want to go to the carnival," she'd whined. "You can even take me there and bring me home if you want to."

When Wyatt had stood his ground, she'd railed at him. "You don't care about me! You never have! All you've ever done is buy me off with presents! Well, not anymore! If you don't let me go tonight, I'll take Mikey and go live with Mom!"

When that threat hadn't worked she'd stormed into her room and slammed the door, something she'd been doing a lot of lately. Wyatt wasn't looking forward to going home and facing her again.

Meanwhile, the snow was calling to him. With so much happening at home, he'd been too busy to ski this season. But some time on the slopes would do him a world of good today. Wyatt kept his own ski gear at the resort. He found himself whistling as he hauled it out of storage. Twenty minutes later he was riding the lift to the top of Breakneck, the resort's steepest run. Pushing off the summit, he flew downhill through the fresh powder, negotiating each rise and turn with the skill that had won him a chestful of Olympic medals. Even after months off, skiing felt as natural to him as walking.

Maybe if Chloe behaved he could bring her along next time. Or, if Leigh chose to stay he could give her lessons. So many *if*s. And they all mattered so much.

The run felt so good that he did it again, and then went down Blackrock, another favorite of his. By the time he finished the sun was low above the mountains and storm clouds were rolling in.

He hadn't meant to stay so late. He would put his gear away and then call Leigh to tell her he was on his way. She'd said something about making spaghetti and garlic bread tonight, so she'd likely be waiting dinner for him.

His office staff had gone home for the day, but the message light was blinking on his phone. He'd call Leigh first, then pick it up.

She answered on the second ring. "Sorry I'm late. I decided to ski," he said. "I'll be home in a few minutes. How's Chloe?"

"I haven't seen her since lunchtime, but I can hear the music blasting in her room. I'm guessing she'll come out when she smells dinner. It'll be ready to dish up when you get here."

"Thanks for waiting. I won't be long." Wyatt wanted to say more, but he knew she wasn't ready to hear it. Instead he ended the call and punched the message button.

"Mr. Richardson." It was Sam Gastineau, head of Security. "There's something you need to be aware of. You can call me on my cell."

Sensing trouble, Wyatt dialed the number. "Sam, what is it?"

"You asked us to monitor your daughter's internet and phone. So far it's been mostly girl talk. But she's been chatting online with an unknown male, and they've arranged a meeting in town."

Wyatt's stomach clenched. "An unknown male? Who?"

"We did some tracing. The name we found is Eric Underhill, which doesn't tell us much. All we've been able to find out so far is that he's not a student at any local high school."

Wyatt's knees threatened to buckle but he knew he had to stay calm. "I'll find out what I can and get back to you," he said.

Hanging up the phone, he dialed his home number again.

Thirteen

Leigh was taking the garlic bread out of the oven when the phone rang a second time. The voice on the line was Wyatt's, but he sounded nothing like the man she'd spoken with a few minutes earlier.

"Leigh, is Chloe there?"

"She's in her room. I can hear—"

"Go and look! If she's there, bring her to the phone!"

Alarmed by the urgency in his voice, she rushed down the hall to Chloe's room. She could hear music through the closed door but there was no reply to her knock. Heart pounding, she turned the knob, swung the door open and froze. The speakers on the computer were blaring. Chloe was nowhere to be seen.

Panic rising, Leigh checked the adjoining bathroom and found it empty. She plunged upstairs and raced from room to room—the nursery where Mikey was sleeping, the guest suites, even the porch. Returning to Chloe's room, she looked for the girl's purse. It was gone. So was her down jacket from the front hall closet.

By the time she got back to the phone she was out of breath. "Wyatt, she's gone! I can't find her anywhere!"

"What about Mikey?" His voice was calm now. Too calm.

"Asleep in his crib. I just saw him." Leigh thought she heard a breath of relief but couldn't be sure. "What is this? What aren't you telling me?"

"I'll explain later. Right now I need you to do one more thing. Open the center drawer in my office desk. In the right front corner you should see a pair of car keys on a black ring. I'll hold on."

She was back in less than a minute, her throat so tight she could barely speak. "No keys. I checked the drawer to make sure they hadn't been moved. They're gone."

After a beat of silence, he muttered something under his breath. "At least I can tell the police what to look for," he said. "Chloe's taken the Bentley."

When Wyatt came outside to the Hummer it was dark. Big, slushy snowflakes tumbled out of the sky, the kind that would freeze on the roads and turn them icy. The Bentley was no good for winter driving. That was why he'd put it away until spring. But Chloe wouldn't have thought of that.

Hellfire, he should've had somebody up to drain the fluids for the winter. That was what he usually did. But with so much on his mind he'd put it off. Now Chloe was driving the vintage sports car and there were so many ways this could end badly.

Not that the Bentley mattered so much. It was just a machine, after all. But his precious daughter wasn't safe in that car. He could only pray that the police would stop her before she hit a patch of icy road.

After talking with Leigh, he'd phoned Sam Gastineau

again and told him to give the police everything they asked for, including the description and license number of the car. According to their emails, Chloe and Eric Underhill, whoever the hell he was, had planned to meet in the school parking lot at the dance. When that hadn't worked out, they'd agreed to try the same place tonight. The whole idea gave Wyatt chills. Who was this person, and why would he want to meet Chloe alone? None of the answers he could think of were good.

Leigh came out on the porch when she heard the Hummer pull up. Wyatt swung out of the vehicle. "Any news?" he asked.

"Nothing. I've been trying to call her cell but she's not answering. Come on inside, it's freezing out here."

"Any idea how long she's been gone?" The glow of the porch light made his haggard face look gray.

Leigh shook her head. "Wyatt, I'm so sorry. If I'd checked on her more often, or tried to get her to talk—"

"It's not your fault." His voice was hoarse with tension. "If anything, it's mine. I should've been more of a father to her over the years. If I had we wouldn't be in this mess." He allowed Leigh to pull him inside and close the door. His hair and sheepskin coat were speckled with wet snow. Leigh suppressed the impulse to wrap her arms around him and hold him. He was too upset for that.

He slumped against the back of the sofa. "My security team's been screening her email. She left to meet someone named Eric Underhill. Have you ever heard the name?"

"Never. It almost sounds made-up."

"I keep trying to sort this out. One thing that's occurred to me is that this Eric Underhill might be Mikey's father."

Leigh flinched as if she'd been struck. Wyatt was guessing, that was all. But what if he was right? What if Kevin had contacted Chloe under another name?

"What if he *is* Mikey's father?" she forced herself to ask. "What would you do?"

"Ask me that after my little girl is safe. The police know where they're supposed to be meeting. They're on their way to pick him up." He raked a hand through his damp hair. "I can't stay here and wait, Leigh. Chloe's out there in the storm in a car that wasn't made for winter roads. And she's on her way to meet a man I know nothing about. I need to be out there looking for her."

Wyatt could be putting himself in danger, too; but Leigh knew better than to argue. "I'll stay here with Mikey," she said. "I've got your cell number. If I hear any news I'll call you. Will you do the same for me?"

"If I can." He pulled her against him in a hard embrace that lasted no more than a heartbeat. Then he turned and strode out the front door. Leigh heard the engine roar and watched the Hummer disappear through the falling snow. With a silent prayer for Wyatt's safety and for Chloe's, she turned and went back into the house.

Fumbling in her purse, she found her cell phone and speed dialed her brother's number. If Kevin was meeting Chloe she had to warn him. A rendezvous between two teenagers wasn't illegal, but once the police learned Kevin's real name, they would surely alert Wyatt, who could be capable of anything tonight.

Her brother's phone rang several times before his voice mail came on. She left a message asking him to call her, then tried her mother's phone. Again, there was no answer.

By now Mikey was awake. Leigh could hear him fussing as she hurried up the stairs. Lifting him from the crib she snuggled him close. His small, warm body was a comfort in her arms.

Kevin could be anywhere, she told herself. Maybe he was at the movies and had turned his phone off. Maybe the battery was low, or he'd left the phone where he couldn't hear it. He probably had nothing to do with Chloe's disappearance. But the two teens had seen each other at the mall. Either of them could have decided to make contact.

Whatever had happened, Leigh sensed that things were about to change. She'd depended on luck to keep her secret. But if Kevin and Chloe were in touch that luck was running out. Wyatt would soon learn the truth—and when he did, the world of love she'd found here would crumble like a sand castle.

The road down the canyon was like an ice rink, so slick that even the Hummer's oversized snow tires found little purchase. Wyatt drove slowly, peering through the thick snowfall for any sign of a wrecked vehicle. With luck the Bentley might just spin off the road. He would find it stuck on the shoulder with Chloe inside, cold and scared but uninjured. Other scenarios that flashed through his mind were much grimmer. She could hit another vehicle or careen into the icy creek below the road. Or she could make it to the rendezvous with Eric Underhill and find herself in more trouble than she'd dreamed of in her worst nightmares.

The highway, when he reached it, was better only in that it was level. In the snowy darkness he could barely see beyond the Hummer's powerful headlights. Had he missed something in the canyon? Should he turn around and look again? Torn, he kept on driving. The police scanner he'd installed in the vehicle was a jumble of static and half-understood voices. He could make out nothing about a wrecked Bentley or a young girl.

If he found her safe things would be different, he

vowed. He would try to be the father she'd missed growing up, and he would be there for Mikey, as well. The
qualified people on his staff could manage the resort just
fine. He could easily take time off to be with his daughter
and grandson—and with Leigh. She'd told him she was
leaving but he hadn't given up on her. If she showed so
much as a spark of feeling for him he would build on that.
He wanted her in his life. He wanted a second chance at
a real family.

Lord, what would he do if the worst happened tonight?

The flash of red and blue lights ahead shocked him out
of his reverie. A cold, sick feeling crept over him as he
glimpsed wreckage through the falling snow.

Swinging onto the shoulder, he braked and vaulted out
of the Hummer. A siren blasted his ears as the ambulance
pulled in from the road. Sprinting closer, Wyatt could see
the rear end of the wrecked car. It lay crumpled on its side
in the barrow pit, its license plate visible in the flashing
lights. He groaned out loud. There was no mistaking the
Bentley.

At first he couldn't see Chloe. Then he spotted her. She
was slumped in the backseat of a police cruiser, her shoulders wrapped in a blanket. Someone next to her was holding a bloodstained towel to her head.

"Chloe!" Wyatt nearly ripped the door off getting it
open. She glanced up and saw him.

"Oh, Daddy!" She was sobbing. "I wrecked your beautiful car. I'm so sorry!"

"It's all right." Wyatt tasted bitter tears. He tried to hug
her but could only reach far enough inside for an awkward
pat. "It's all right, honey," he muttered again. "It's only
a car. You're okay, sweetheart—that's all that matters."

An officer had come up behind him. "Looks like she
slid off and rolled," he said. "The worst part was, nobody

saw it happen. She was conscious when we found her, but she must've been in that car, trapped by her seat belt, for a good forty minutes before a patrolman came by and called it in."

Wyatt's gut clenched as he thought of his daughter, helpless, bleeding, cold and alone. What if no one had found her? She could have died by the time he got here.

The paramedics had eased Chloe out of the car, wrapped her in warm blankets and laid her on a stretcher. "We'll know more once we get her to the hospital," one of them told Wyatt. "But I'm guessing she's in shock, maybe some hypothermia, too. The head gash isn't as deep as it looks but she's lost a fair amount of blood."

Wyatt squeezed Chloe's hand as they loaded her into the back of the ambulance. "I'll be right behind you," he said. "Hang in there, honey, you're going to be fine."

He was headed back to the Hummer when another officer stopped him. "We just got a call, Mr. Richardson. They've arrested the man who was waiting for her at the school. He's a forty-year-old construction worker with an assault record. Her emails were on his phone. Your girl was lucky twice tonight."

"Thanks." Wyatt felt his knees begin to buckle as the policeman walked away. He made it to his vehicle, slid onto the seat, rested his head on the steering wheel and shook with emotion.

The ambulance was pulling back onto the road. Starting the engine he followed the taillights through the swirling snow.

Leigh would be waiting for his call. He could always phone her from the hospital when he knew more about Chloe's condition. But Wyatt knew he couldn't delay that long. Right now, more than anything, he needed to hear her voice.

* * *

Leigh had fed Mikey and was sitting on the upstairs sofa with him. She'd turned the TV to the local news, praying not to see a wreck or an arrest, but compelled to watch anyway. Wyatt had been gone less than an hour. It could turn out to be a long night.

Mikey had just dozed off when the ringing phone startled him awake. Her pulse lurched when she saw Wyatt's name on the caller ID. Bracing for the worst she picked up.

"Wyatt, what's happened?"

"I found Chloe." Leigh could sense the relief in his voice. "She rolled the car, but she doesn't seem too badly hurt. I'm following the ambulance now. We'll know more when they get her to the hospital."

"Thank heaven!" She sank into the cushions as the tension drained from her body. Chloe was safe, at least. But was that the whole story? Was Kevin out there in the storm, waiting for her in the school parking lot? Had the police picked him up? Leigh had tried her brother's phone again and again with no answer. Her mother wasn't answering, either.

"What about the person Chloe was meeting?" she asked. "Eric Underhill, or whatever his name was?"

"The police arrested the bastard. He's forty years old, a predator who connects with young girls in teen chat rooms. Lord, Leigh, Chloe could've been raped, kidnapped, even murdered. I've never believed in guardian angels, but that wreck likely saved her."

Leigh succumbed to a rush of scalding tears. Chloe was all right. Kevin hadn't been involved. Her secret was safe. But for how long?

"Leigh, are you there?"

"Yes," she whispered past the lump in her throat.

"I'll call you again when I know more about Chloe. For now I just wanted to give you the news."

"Thank you." She paused. "Be careful, Wyatt. And tell Chloe we love her."

There was no reply. He'd ended the call.

Lifting Mikey against her shoulder, Leigh kissed his silky head. His fingers closed around a button on her shirt, clasping tight. He was so precious—so wise in his own baby way. Leaving him would tear out a piece of her heart.

She loved all three of them, Leigh realized—Mikey. His vulnerable young mother, whose journey to womanhood was so fraught with struggle. And Wyatt, who'd do anything to protect and provide for those closest to him. Tonight, in his voice, she'd sensed the fear, the anger and finally the relief. Beneath that flinty exterior was a tender man who cared deeply for others. A man who needed her.

When she'd taken this job she'd warned herself to guard her emotions. But this troubled family had drawn her into their embrace. They had won her love.

And her lie would betray them all.

Tell Chloe we love her.

Leigh's words, which he'd barely caught, came back to Wyatt as he walked into the hospital room. Chloe lay propped in the bed, her hair a splash of color against the bleached pillowcase. A white gauze patch was taped to her forehead where the doctor had made stitches. A monitor above the bed beeped out her vital signs.

She gave him a wan smile. "Hi, Daddy."

"Hi, sweetheart." He squeezed her foot, fearful of hurting her if he touched her anyplace else. "How are you feeling?"

"Not so great, but better than before. I heard about the

man the police caught. He sent me this cute photo and told me he was eighteen. I did a stupid thing, didn't I?"

"Yes, you did. You're lucky to be alive. But we'll talk about that later."

"How's the Bentley? I know you loved that car."

"I'll look at the car tomorrow. Right now the only thing that matters is that you're safe. The doctor says you don't have a concussion, but they want to keep you here overnight. They'll give you something to help you sleep. And I'll be right here in case you need anything."

"Daddy." She held out her hand. Stepping forward he took it. Her fingers were warm from the heated blankets. His were cold.

"I'm a big girl, and the nurses are taking good care of me. You don't need to be here. Go home to Leigh and Mikey. Get some rest."

"You're certain you won't need me?"

Her fingers tightened. "Please, Daddy, you look so tired. I'll be fine here."

"If you're sure." He moved toward the door, then hesitated as Leigh's last words came back to him.

Tell Chloe we love her.

When was the last time he'd told her that? Could he even remember?

He walked back to the bed, bent and kissed her cheek. "I love you, Chloe. So do Leigh and Mikey."

"I love you, too, Daddy." Were there tears in her eyes? "Now go get some rest. I'll be fine."

When he walked out to the parking lot the snow was still falling. The Hummer was blanketed in white. Wyatt turned on the defrosters and brushed off the mirrors and windows. It was after midnight and he was exhausted. But he felt as if a burden had been lifted. His beloved daughter was safe and had hopefully learned a lesson. Maybe they could turn a corner from here.

Plowing through the drifts, he backed out of the parking lot and onto the road. He'd called Leigh a couple of hours ago and told her he planned to stay at the hospital. Since she didn't expect him home, she'd probably gone to bed.

He imagined her asleep, her eyes closed, her hair like a pool of dark silk against the pillowcase. He imagined lying beside her, inhaling the sweet, warm aroma that cloaked her skin. A hunger stirred and rose in him. He needed her, wanted her with an ache that could only be satisfied in one way.

She'd rejected him before. If she rejected him now, that would be the end of it. He was laying his pride on the line, but that was a chance he had to take.

He didn't want to be alone tonight.

Fourteen

Lying awake in the darkness, Leigh heard the Hummer pull into the garage. She'd gone to bed soon after Wyatt's second call, but sleep had refused to come. Without the presence of its owner the house was like a vast, empty cavern—too large and too quiet.

She missed his voice and the sound of his footsteps. She missed sitting beside him while the evening news played out and watching him cuddle Mikey. She missed his laughter, the clean spicy aroma of his skin, and the sense of homecoming when his arms were around her.

Get used to it, Leigh, she'd admonished herself. *Get used to life without him, because that's the only life you'll ever have.*

She'd known all along that when the time came, she'd have to move on. But it would be harder than she'd ever imagined.

Curled in the downy featherbed, she'd listened for what seemed like hours to the howling wind and the snow pelting the windowpanes. She'd told herself that Wyatt's choice to stay at the hospital with Chloe had been a wise one. Even for a brawny vehicle like his, the blinding storm could be dangerous. On the steep mountain road it would be all too easy to overshoot a curve and go crashing down the slope.

Yet—unless she was hearing things—he'd just driven all the way home. Why? she suddenly wondered. Was something wrong?

Bounding out of bed, she threw her flannel robe over the outsized T-shirt she wore for sleep. Barefoot, she pattered down the stairs. She could hear the faint sound of a snow shovel scraping the walkway from the garage to the house. As she reached the entry, the door opened, letting in a blast of snow and icy air.

Wyatt stepped across the threshold and closed the door behind him. Snow clung to his boots, his hair, his eyebrows and the stubble on his chin. As Leigh stood shivering, he flung off his gloves, unzipped his parka and opened the front. "Come here, Leigh," he said.

For an instant she stared at him as if he'd lost his mind. Then, in the glow of the entry light, she caught the twinkle in his eyes.

She flung herself across the space between them, her arms wrapping his rib cage through the woolen sweater. He closed the front flaps of his coat, enfolding her in his warmth.

"Damn, but you feel good," he muttered.

She tilted her gaze upward. "What are you doing back here?" she scolded. "It's a mess out there. I thought you were staying at the hospital."

He chuckled. "I was. Chloe sent me home. Smart girl."

"Can I make you some coffee? Or maybe some hot cocoa to warm you up?"

"I've had enough coffee to sink a battleship. As for

warming me up…I can think of something better than cocoa."

His tone was light, almost joking. But Leigh sensed an undertone of vulnerability. The man had driven home through a Colorado blizzard because he wanted to make love to her. He had placed his heart and his manly pride in her hands. How could she not love him for that?

She hadn't counted on this. But whatever the consequences, there was no way on earth she would deny him.

Stretching on tiptoe she caught his head and pulled him down to her in a long, intimate kiss. By the time it ended they were both breathing hard. Stepping back, she opened his coat and slid it off his shoulders. He reached down and managed to work off his boots. "Fair warning," he said. "I'm chilled to the bone."

"I think I can deal with that." She took his hand and led him toward the stairs.

In the glow of the night-light, Wyatt shed his clothes next to her bed. Still wearing her long gray T-shirt, she slid between the sheets and made room for him. "Come on in, I left you a warm spot," she whispered. Naked and shivering, he slipped into the bed and into her open arms.

Laughing, she pulled him close. "Brrr…you've got goose bumps," she teased.

"I thought you said you could deal with that." Their legs were deliciously tangled, her T-shirt already bunched above her waist. She wore nothing underneath. How could such an ordinary garment be so sexy? He tried to avoid touching her bare skin with his chilled hands, but she took them, slid them under her shirt and cupped the palms over her breasts. Soon they were very, very warm.

By now he was aroused to the point of bursting. Luckily he always kept protection in his wallet, which was still in his jeans. The time he'd slept with Leigh in the hotel had been like a Hollywood production he'd stage-managed. This time was like...just plain lovemaking—sweet, spontaneous, real, and so damned good he could hardly stand it. He wanted this. He wanted it every night of his life.

He kissed her mouth and her lovely face, sucked her nipples and stroked her nub until she dripped with moisture. Then he mounted her eager hips and thrust home where it felt as if he'd always belonged. She made a little purring sound as his swollen length filled her. "Are you warm enough now?" she teased.

"Warm and getting warmer." He withdrew and glided in again, watching the expressions flicker across her face. Making love to Leigh was a whole new world, as much emotional as it was physical. It was a deep sharing, almost as if he could feel what she was feeling, as if her pleasure was his—and he knew it was because he loved her.

He loved her and he never wanted to let her go.

When his male urge became too strong to hold back, he drove into her hard. She arched her hips to meet his thrusts, hands gripping his buttocks, pulling him deeper as sensations crested. She came with a shudder and a soft cry. He clasped her close as his release burst.

Spent, now, he buried his face in the damp cleft between her breasts. Bathed in her sweet, musky woman smell, he lay still as her fingers wove tender paths through his hair. Earlier they'd been joking, making light of their need for each other. Now, for the moment, neither of them could speak.

Shifting to one side he brushed a kiss onto her ripe, damp mouth. "Warm now," he murmured. She replied with a misty smile and moved over to give him more space. The last thing he remembered that night was drifting off in her arms.

* * *

Mikey woke, as usual, in the early dawn. Attuned to the little sounds he made, Leigh slipped out of the warm bed, hurried into the adjoining room and scooped him up before he could cry and wake Wyatt. He gurgled and butted his head against her shoulder, then settled for chomping on her shirt while his bottle warmed.

She put him down long enough to change his diaper. Then, cradling him against her shoulder, she wandered back into her bedroom. Wyatt lay bathed in soft gray light, one arm flung outward over the spot where she'd slept. His eyes were closed, his hair appealingly tousled, his jaw shadowed with stubble. Asleep, he looked so sexy he took her breath away.

Last night in his arms had been pure heaven. But making love with Wyatt had only sunk her deeper into the morass of lies she'd created. Whether she wanted to or not, it was time to start planning her exit strategy.

Returning to the nursery, she took the bottle out of the warmer, found a blanket to cover her legs and settled in the rocker with Mikey. He drank hungrily, making little squeaks as he swallowed—just one of the baby sounds she'd grown to love. Maybe someday she'd have a baby of her own. But that wouldn't be in the picture anytime soon.

She'd given her two weeks' notice and time was running out. But as far as she knew, Wyatt wasn't taking applications for her replacement. Maybe this time he'd decided to go through an agency. Either way, she couldn't allow that to be her problem. Chloe could take care of her baby if need be, or they could bring in Dora.

She'd planned to stay a few more days; but last night with Wyatt in her bed had complicated everything. The sooner she got out of here the less damage would be left in her wake.

Mikey had finished his bottle. Draping a clean cloth on her shoulder, Leigh boosted him upright and patted his back. For a moment she pressed her cheek against his firm little body. As his sweet baby smell filled her senses, tears welled in her eyes. Everything she'd ever wanted was right here in this house. And she had no choice except to walk away from it all.

Wyatt opened his eyes to find her gone. Half-awake, he felt a surge of panic. Then he came to his senses and saw the light from the nursery. Of course, she'd be in there with Mikey. "Leigh?" he called.

"Right here." She stood in the open doorway, wearing nothing but that gray T-shirt that skimmed the edge of indecency. Too bad she was holding the baby.

"Come on back to bed," he said. "That's an order."

"All right. But I'll have to bring Mikey with me. He slept through the night and he's wide-awake. He won't stand for being put back in his crib."

"Fine." As she crossed the floor Wyatt punched up the pillows and turned down the duvet. He'd slept soundly last night, but not *all* night. Sometime in the wee hours he'd awakened. With Leigh's silky warmth nestled against him, he'd gazed up into the darkness, thinking.

There was no way he could let this beautiful woman walk out of his life. If Leigh was still planning to leave, he had to stop her any way he could.

She'd bridled at the suggestion that she remain as his lover. That, in fact, was when she'd announced she was quitting her job. But would she say no to a wedding ring?

Wyatt had resisted the whole idea of marriage for years. He'd been there, done that, and it hadn't worked out. He had one child, and he hadn't done a great job with her.

Why take a chance again—especially with a younger wife who'd likely want children of her own?

But the woman sleeping beside him had made a hash of his objections. He loved her. He wanted her for keeps. For so long, marriage had sounded like nothing more than a trap—but now it was the prize he wanted desperately to win, as long as he could have it with her.

She walked toward the bed, carrying Mikey in her arms. Mussed and tousled, her face bare of makeup, she was still a goddess with the power to take his breath away.

Easing into bed, she pulled the covers up and laid Mikey on top, in the warm hollow between their bodies. Mikey gurgled happily and kicked his feet, clearly liking where he was.

Wyatt gave the boy's tummy a playful tickle. It felt natural, lying in bed with a baby between them, even if the baby was not technically theirs.

Leigh had settled on her side, her head on the pillow and a sleepy smile on her face. "What time are you picking up Chloe?"

"I'll want to be there early. But if the doctor is slow checking her out I may be a while."

"What are you going to do with her, Wyatt? The girl has a child to raise. And you almost lost her last night. She can't keep acting out like this."

"I know." Wyatt shook his head. It wasn't Chloe he'd planned to talk about this morning. "Maybe some counseling, even rehab if her drinking is out of control. But Chloe has to want help. Otherwise it won't work." He drew a shaky breath. "I wish you'd consider staying, Leigh. Chloe and Mikey need you. I need you. You've become family."

"That's exactly why I should leave." She reached across Mikey and laid a gentle hand on Wyatt's arm. "Don't you see? Things are becoming complicated. The longer I stay, the more painful it will be when I have to go."

"You don't have to go at all." He captured her hand in his, searching for the right words. "I know I've got some issues. My father was an alcoholic who abused my mother and me before he died in prison. We were so poor we barely had enough to eat. I never learned what it meant to be a good husband and father. I thought that if I provided for Tina and Chloe financially and didn't hurt them, that was all I needed to do. But I'm learning how wrong I was—learning it every day from Chloe, Mikey and you. Learning how to do it better this time."

He saw a moist glimmer in her eyes. She blinked and it was gone.

"Marry me, Leigh," he said. "I know I'm supposed to do this on my knees with a diamond ring in my hand, but I'm afraid that if I wait you might be gone—and I can't stand the thought of losing you."

Feeling as if he'd just stuck a knife in his gut, Wyatt waited. He could sense her hesitation. Even before she spoke he knew what her answer would be.

"This isn't a good time," she said. "I'm sorry, Wyatt. If things were different you know what my answer would be. But I can't stay. I just…can't." Her voice had begun to break. She pressed her lips together.

"You could at least tell me why."

"No." She emphasized the word with a shake of her head. "Don't even ask me."

"Well…" He threw up a stone wall to hide his devastation. "You can't blame a man for trying. I guess it's time for me to go downstairs and get ready for the day." He swung out of bed, gathered up his clothes and strode toward the door.

"Wyatt, I'm sorry, I—"

He glanced back at her. She looked as if she were about to cry, but he couldn't let himself care. "Don't," he growled. "You've already said enough."

Leigh stood with Mikey at the nursery window, watching the Hummer pull out of the driveway. Now would be the time to leave, before he returned with Chloe. But the roads weren't plowed yet and she couldn't leave Mikey here alone. She had little choice except to wait for her chance later in the day.

But one thing was certain. Her time here had run out.

She bathed Mikey, reminding herself it was for the last time. He chortled and splashed, loving the feel of the warm water. When she wrapped him in his towel he snuggled close, his head resting against her throat. As she held him, the tears came, hot and bitter, trickling down her cheeks. She'd known this time would come, but she wasn't prepared for its impact. She would never see Mikey's first step or hear his first spoken word. She wouldn't see him off to school or help him with his homework. She would love him forever, but he wasn't hers to keep. And neither was his handsome, sexy grandfather.

By the time she'd dressed him and brushed his hair into a curl at the peak of his adorable head, he was hungry again. Leigh fed him and put him down for a nap. Then, as if to convince herself she was really leaving, she dragged her suitcase out of the closet. Her thoughts churned as she packed.

Wyatt deserved far better than what she'd given him. This morning he'd been honest with her. He'd laid his heart on the line and she'd tossed it away. All the while she'd been in torment, knowing she had no choice except to hurt him.

He and Chloe had taken her into their home and treated

her like family. They'd trusted her completely. It was time she faced up to her lies. No matter how risky, the very least she owed them was the truth.

Packing done, she closed her suitcase and slid it back into the closet. Then with a pad of resort stationery and a pen borrowed from Wyatt's office, she sat at the dressing table in her room and slowly, painfully, began to write.

By the time the doctor showed up to check Chloe out of the hospital it was midmorning. Sunlight blazed in a clear blue sky. The skiing would be glorious today. But Wyatt's mood didn't match the weather.

He'd always thought himself a good judge of people, but he'd misread Leigh by a mile. Last night their love-making had been so good. He'd felt so close to her. But this morning she'd rejected him without a second thought.

He'd asked her to marry him! Did she think he did that with every woman he met? He'd bared his soul to her, hoping she'd do the same. But she'd rejected his proposal without even telling him why. He ought to be furious. Instead he was just plain, damned miserable.

What was driving her away from him? A scandalous past? Legal or health issues? A returning lover? The difference in their ages? Maybe she just didn't love him. Knowing the truth might at least make her refusal easier to accept. But Leigh had locked the door on her secret. It was driving him crazy.

"You're awfully quiet this morning, Daddy." Chloe sat beside him, buckled into the high seat. She was sound enough to go home, but the gash on her forehead would take time to heal.

"You've been pretty quiet yourself," he said.

"I was waiting for you to start lecturing me."

"Aside from being grateful you're alive, all I can say is, I hope you've learned your lesson."

"You mean the one about driving a sports car in a blizzard to meet some psycho creep who found me on the internet? Sure I have. But I still have a lot to learn."

Wyatt focused his attention on the road. He sensed that she had more to say. Was he ready to hear it?

"I did a lot of thinking in the hospital," she said. "When I first decided to keep Mikey, it was because I wanted someone all my own to love. But I didn't understand what it took to be a mother. I wasn't ready, Daddy. I'm still not ready. I proved that last night. All I wanted was somebody to pay attention to me, and it almost got me killed."

Wyatt felt his heart drop. "What are you saying?"

Her hands twisted in her lap. "I love Mikey. But the most loving thing I can do is give him a responsible mom. Leigh's been more of a mother to him than I have."

"Leigh's leaving. You know that. Are you saying you'd give Mikey up?"

"I was kind of hoping you could get married and adopt him. You could even marry Leigh."

Wyatt stared ahead at the freshly plowed canyon road. "I already asked her, honey. She said no."

"Oh." The girl fell silent. Neither of them spoke as the Hummer climbed the last mile to the house. The snow-draped pines and azure sky made the setting look like a Christmas card. But today Wyatt saw everything in shades of gray. Not only was he losing Leigh; there was a chance he could lose Mikey, too.

Leigh wasn't at the door to meet them, but the sound of footsteps and water running upstairs told him she was there. With Chloe settled in her room, he ordered pizza and a salad from the resort and went into his office to catch up on some work. Leigh was probably avoiding him. Fine. For now he would spare her the discomfort.

An hour later, when lunch arrived, there was still no sign of Leigh. Wyatt was debating whether to seek her out when Chloe came downstairs with the baby in her arms.

"Where's Leigh?" Wyatt asked her.

"She went down to the resort on some kind of errand. She left me the baby monitor and said to listen for Mikey."

"She took the Mercedes?"

Chloe shrugged. "I guess. I didn't see her go."

Wyatt couldn't explain the feeling that came over him. But somehow he sensed what had happened. Pushing past Chloe, he dashed upstairs and raced down the hall to Leigh's room. Everything was in perfect order. The bed was neatly made. The closet and dresser drawers were closed. But when he looked inside, they were empty. All of Leigh's things were gone.

Fighting despair, he scanned the room, looking for anything that might tell him more. He found it in the form of a sealed envelope sticking out from under the pillow. His name was printed on the outside.

Tearing it open, he sank onto the bed and began reading the handwritten pages.

Fifteen

Dear Wyatt,
I know you won't like my leaving this way, but I
didn't have the courage to face you and say goodbye. I'll be picking up my old car at the resort. Your
Mercedes will be waiting for you there, with the keys
at the front desk.

Leigh's handwriting was as delicate, precise and femi-
nine as she was. Wyatt fought the urge to crumple the
pages in his fist and fling them against the wall. He'd believed in her. He'd offered her everything he had. How
could she do this?

You and Chloe took me into your home and gave
me your trust. I repaid that trust with a lie. Now that
I'm leaving, you're entitled to the truth. I applied for
this job under false pretenses. I wanted to be your
nanny because Mikey is my nephew. His father is
my seventeen-year-old brother.

Wyatt stared at the page, feeling as if he'd been knocked flat on his back. He'd been suspicious of Leigh's motives from the beginning—at least until he'd fallen under her spell. But the connection to Mikey had never crossed his mind. How could he have been so blind? Why hadn't he guessed the obvious?

Leigh could have confessed at any time. After all, she'd broken no law. Why had she kept her secret so long?

The next paragraph held the answer to that question.

I hid the truth to save my job, and to protect my brother, a good boy with a promising future. Now I'm begging you not to take your anger out on him. When Chloe informed him she was pregnant, he offered to take responsibility. But she told him she didn't plan to keep the baby. He has no idea that Chloe changed her mind. He knows nothing about Mikey. Neither does my mother.

Under the terms of the nondisclosure agreement, I don't plan to tell them. I'm hoping you won't, either. But that decision should rightly be left to Chloe.

When I saw your ad at the paper I suspected the baby was my brother's child. I couldn't be sure at first. But when I held him all doubt vanished.

My only motive in taking the nanny job was to know my little nephew and help get him off to a loving start. He has that start. Now it's time for me to step out of his life—and yours. Mikey will have no memory of me. But I hope that some part of him will recall how much he was loved.

Chloe loves him, too, I know. She has a lot to learn, but she has it in her to be a wonderful mother.

With your help and support, she will get there and make something good of her life.

As for you and me, Wyatt, there are no words. If things had been different…but there's no use going there. I can only hope that one day you'll understand and forgive me.
Leigh

Leigh drove the rusty station wagon toward town, her eyes burning with unshed tears. By now Wyatt had probably found her letter and read it. He would be shocked, hurt and angry. She could only hope he'd respect her wishes, and Chloe's, and leave Kevin alone.

Would he ever forgive her? Wyatt was a proud man. She had lied to him, deceived him and rejected his offer of love. If he hated her for the rest of his life, it would be no worse than she deserved.

She was headed home for now. But there was no way she could stay in Dutchman's Creek. Tonight she would call her friend Christine in Denver and arrange to bunk on her couch while she found an apartment and a job. Then she'd pack her car and leave in the morning. At least the nanny gig had paid well enough for a new start. Too bad she couldn't afford to give Wyatt's money back. She'd never felt right about taking the generous salary under false pretenses. Maybe someday she'd be able to repay him.

How would Chloe feel when she learned the truth? Leigh had grown to care for Wyatt's high-spirited daughter. But any future contact between them would be out of the question. And Mikey? She couldn't even think about him now—or about Wyatt. For the past few weeks they'd been her life. Now it was time to put that life behind her.

* * *

Chloe finished reading Leigh's letter. Her calm reaction was the last thing Wyatt had expected. "You don't seem surprised," he said.

"I'm not."

"You *knew?*"

"Not 100 percent. But I was pretty sure. The last name was a clue. She looked like her brother, too—same coloring, same build, same eyes. And no stranger could've loved Mikey the way she did. I could tell that right off. It was like she would've fought man-eating tigers to protect him."

They were on the living room sofa. Wyatt had taken Mikey and was holding the boy on his lap while she read the letter. "Why didn't you say something?" he asked her.

"I liked her, and she was so good with Mikey. I was afraid if I confronted her about it, she'd leave or that you'd fire her and we'd have to find a different nanny." She laid the letter on the coffee table. "I was even more afraid that you might go after Kevin and hurt him."

"Kevin? That's his name?" Wyatt felt his jaw tighten.

"Kevin Foster. He goes to Public. But it wasn't really his fault, Daddy. We were at this big party, everybody was kind of drunk, and I was looking at him because he was cute. We got talking and one thing led to another. We used protection but it…broke."

Wyatt glanced down at Mikey, who was trying to eat a button on his sweater. "Good Lord, Chloe, what were you thinking?"

"That's just it. I wasn't." She gave a little sob. "I just wanted somebody to pay attention to me. The next day I felt so stupid that I decided I never wanted to see him again. Leigh was being honest in her letter—Kevin really did try to be there for me, up until I told him I was getting rid of the baby. I didn't want him to be involved. But look what I ended up with—the sweetest little baby ever!"

And now you don't know what to do with him, Wyatt thought, but he knew better than to say it out loud.

"Would you have gone after Kevin, Daddy? Would you have hurt him?"

Wyatt exhaled, feeling the tension leave his body. "I wanted to at first. But what's done is done, and now we've got Mikey. All we can do now is forgive the past and do whatever's best for him."

"If Leigh had known you felt like that, do you think she would have left?"

He shrugged, his emotions still numb. "Who knows? She's gone."

"So why don't we find her and ask her?"

Wyatt stared at his daughter.

"Think about it, Daddy," she said. "Leigh is the best thing that ever happened to you—and to Mikey. Don't you think it's worth another try to get her back?" Standing, she lifted the baby from his arms. "Have your security goons find out where her family lives. Mikey and I will come with you. She can't say no to all three of us."

"I still don't understand why you have to leave town so soon." Leigh's mother ladled steaming homemade chili into three bowls. "Are you in some kind of trouble?"

Leigh glanced up from slicing bread. She was sick and tired of secrets. But keeping the truth from her family was a necessary kindness. "I told you the reason," she said, hating the lie. "When I talked to Christine she told me about a job opening at an ad agency. The deadline's tomorrow and I have to apply in person."

"But surely there are jobs here in Dutchman's Creek.

What happened with that nanny job, anyway? Did you get caught stealing the family silver?"

"Leigh had a nanny job?" Kevin had just come in from shoveling snow and was taking his boots off in the entry. "So that was the secret agent gig? How come I never heard about it?"

"I suppose I can tell you now." Leigh's mother spoke up before Leigh could hush her. "Your sister had a job baby-sitting for some big-name celebrity. But she couldn't tell me who it was."

"I still can't," Leigh added. "I had to sign a nondisclosure agreement."

"But they had a baby," her mother said. "I could hear the little thing crying over the phone."

"Let me guess." Kevin grinned as he pulled off his gloves. "Movie stars? Rock stars?"

"Guess away." Leigh tossed a pot holder at him. "Guess all night if you want. I still can't tell you."

"You might not have to." Kevin glanced out the front window. "You know that fancy SUV you were driving last time you came home? It just pulled up in front of the house."

The bread knife Leigh was using clattered to the kitchen floor. Her first impulse was to flee to the bathroom and lock herself in. But that would only make her look foolish. Whatever business Wyatt had here, she had no choice except to stay where she was and brazen it out.

From the kitchen, Leigh couldn't see the front window. But she could see her brother. He was staring outside. His face had gone ashen. "Oh, my God," he muttered.

"What on earth…?" Their mother set the pan back on the stove. Wiping her hands on her apron, she bustled toward the sound of the doorbell. Leigh strode into the living room and seized Kevin's hand, gripping hard. Whatever they had to face, they would face it together.

The door swung open. Chloe stood on the threshold with Mikey in her arms and her father a step behind her. A ski hat hid the bandage on her head. "Hello, Mrs. Foster," she said. "My name is Chloe Richardson, and this is my son, Michael. My father and I are here to talk to Leigh."

Leigh glanced at Kevin. He looked ready to faint. Her own legs felt unsteady, but she couldn't help admiring Chloe. The girl had stepped right up.

Chloe had said nothing about Mikey being Kevin's child. But Kevin would know. Only their mother remained in the dark. She smiled and greeted the visitors as she ushered them into the living room. Leigh was about to speak up when Kevin stepped forward.

"Why didn't you tell me about him, Chloe?" he demanded. "Didn't you think I'd want to know I had a son, and that you'd kept him?"

Chloe met his scowl with a level gaze. "I'm here, Kevin. Right now that's the best I can do."

Mikey's wise blue eyes took in the stranger who was his father. Kevin's anger crumbled into glimmering tears. "Can I hold him?" he asked.

"Here." She passed him the baby. "Careful, you'll need to support his head."

Kevin held his son as if he were made of spun glass. A tear spilled out of his eye and trickled down his cheek. His mother had sunk onto the sofa. Joining her, Leigh slipped a supporting arm around her shoulders. "I'm sorry," she whispered. "I wanted to tell you, but I couldn't."

Kevin turned toward the sofa. "Here's your grandson, Mom. Do you want to hold him?"

"Oh! Oh, my goodness!" She held out her arms and gathered Mikey close. He responded to her warmth and sure touch by snuggling against her chest. She began to weep softly.

Wyatt had remained in the entry, silent as he watched the drama unfold. Now he crossed the room and stopped in front of them. "Mrs. Foster," he said, "If you'll excuse us, I need to talk to Leigh. Alone."

Leaving the others to sort things out, Leigh led him into the small kitchen, closed the door and braced for a storm. "Say anything you want, Wyatt," she said, facing him from across the table. "Call me ugly names, threaten to sue me. But you're not getting an apology. I regret having to lie to you and Chloe. I regret hurting your pride. But my time with Mikey was worth any price I have to pay now."

"And the two of us?" Something hidden flickered in his gaze. "What about that?"

"Don't." She looked away to hide her welling tears. "I don't regret falling in love with you. But I know what I've done. I know that whatever we had, I've ruined it all."

"You fell in love with me?" A smile tugged at a corner of his mouth.

"Don't tell me you're surprised. How could any woman *not* fall in love with you? But what difference does it make? I lied to you. I lied to Chloe."

"Listen to me, Leigh." He strode around the table and seized her hands. His clasp was gentle but she sensed that if she tried to pull away his grip would turn to steel. "Chloe guessed your secret early on. She didn't say anything because she saw how much you loved Mikey, and she wanted you to stay."

Leigh stared at him. Her lips trembled.

"We *both* want you to stay," he said. "Chloe did some very grown-up thinking overnight. She knows she's not ready to be a mother. What she wants is for you and me to adopt Mikey and raise him as our son. For that, I think we need to be married. But above and beyond that, I want to marry you because I love you, and hope to spend the rest of my life with you. So I'm asking you one more time, will you marry me, Leigh? Will you let me spoil you and love you and need you every day for the rest of our lives?"

The tears broke through, streaming in salty rivulets down her cheeks. "Yes," she whispered. "Yes, with all my heart."

He fished out a clean handkerchief and blotted her face. "Well, then," he murmured. "Should we go in the other room and break the news?"

"Not so fast, mister!" Laughing now, she flung her arms around his neck. Their deep, heartfelt kiss lasted a very long time.

Epilogue

Two years later
May

"Mikey, come back here!" Leigh grabbed for her active two-year-old son, but she wasn't fast enough. He ducked under the row of seats and scampered into the center aisle. From there he made a beeline toward the front of the auditorium, where the organist was just beginning "Pomp and Circumstance."

"Stay put. I'll cut him off at the pass." Wyatt slipped out of his seat and circled around the outside aisle. He reached the little fugitive and snatched him up just short of the steps to the stage. With Mikey in a vise grip, he regained his seat. "I'm getting too old for this," he muttered into his wife's ear.

Glancing at her rounded belly, Leigh gave him a grin. "Just wait till his little sister gets here," she whispered. "Then we'll really have our hands full. For now, let's see how long we can keep him quiet."

Wyatt fished a toy rabbit out of his pocket, then turned to watch as the Bramford Hill graduates paraded down the aisle.

Chloe was third in line, her head high and proud, her fiery curls spilling from under her white cap. In the past two years she'd matured into a responsible, confident young woman. Now she was graduating with honors and had been accepted into the prelaw program at a prestigious eastern college. Wyatt couldn't have been more proud of her.

It was a shame her mother wasn't here. Tina had sent a card and a generous check. But she was living in Paris now, with her wealthy third husband. This time, so far, she seemed happy.

Kevin, who'd graduated two years ago, was majoring in physics at the University of Colorado. He and Chloe kept in touch as friends, but life was taking them on different paths, which was as it should be. They would always have Mikey as an anchor.

As for Mikey, he would grow up with Leigh and Wyatt as his parents, Chloe as his big sister, and Kevin as his uncle. He'd be told the truth when he grew old enough to understand. For now it was enough that the little boy was part of a family, and that they loved him.

As Chloe crossed the stage to get her diploma, Wyatt's thoughts drifted back to the day he'd opened the door to see her standing on the porch, forlorn and pregnant. Little had he realized, in his dismay, that heaven was about to open up and shower untold blessings on his head.

Leigh, Mikey, his unborn baby daughter and a fresh start with Chloe—everything had come from that day. And as he clasped his son close and slipped an arm around his wife, all Wyatt could do was be grateful.

* * * * *

#2281 HER TEXAN TO TAME

Lone Star Legacy • by Sara Orwig

The wide-open space of the Delaney's Texas ranch is the perfect place for chef Jessica to forget her past. But when the rugged ranch boss's flirtations become serious, the heat is undeniable!

#2282 WHAT A RANCHER WANTS

Texas Cattleman's Club: The Missing Mogul
by Sarah M. Anderson

Chance McDaniel knows what he wants when he sees it, and he wants Gabriella. But while this Texas rancher is skilled at seduction, he never expects the virginal Gabriella to capture his heart.

#2283 SNOWBOUND WITH A BILLIONAIRE

Billionaires and Babies • by Jules Bennett

Movie mogul Max Ford returns home, only to get snowed-in with his ex—and her baby! This time, Max will fight for the woman he lost—even as the truth tears them apart.

#2284 BACK IN HER HUSBAND'S BED

by Andrea Laurence

Nathan and his estranged wife, poker champion Annie, agree to play the happy couple to uncover cheating at his casino. But their bluff lands her back in her husband's bed—for good this time?

#2285 JUST ONE MORE NIGHT

The Pearl House • by Fiona Brand

Riveted by Elena's transformation from charming duckling into seriously sexy swan, Aussie Nick Messena wants one night with her. But soon Nick realizes one night will never be enough....

#2286 BOUND BY A CHILD

Baby Business • by Katherine Garbera

When their best friends leave them guardians of a baby girl, business rivals Allan and Jessi call a truce. But an unexpected attraction changes the terms of this merger.

HDCNM0114

REQUEST YOUR FREE BOOKS!
2 FREE NOVELS PLUS 2 FREE GIFTS!

⊞HARLEQUIN®

Desire

ALWAYS POWERFUL, PASSIONATE AND PROVOCATIVE

YES! Please send me 2 FREE Harlequin Desire® novels and my 2 FREE gifts (gifts are worth about $10). After receiving them, if I don't wish to receive any more books, I can return the shipping statement marked "cancel." If I don't cancel, I will receive 6 brand-new novels every month and be billed just $4.55 per book in the U.S. or $4.99 per book in Canada. That's a savings of at least 13% off the cover price! It's quite a bargain! Shipping and handling is just 50¢ per book in the U.S. and 75¢ per book in Canada.* I understand that accepting the 2 free books and gifts places me under no obligation to buy anything. I can always return a shipment and cancel at any time. Even if I never buy another book, the two free books and gifts are mine to keep forever.

225/326 HDN F4ZC

Name	(PLEASE PRINT)	
Address		Apt. #
City	State/Prov.	Zip/Postal Code

Signature (if under 18, a parent or guardian must sign)

Mail to the **Harlequin®** Reader Service:
IN U.S.A.: P.O. Box 1867, Buffalo, NY 14240-1867
IN CANADA: P.O. Box 609, Fort Erie, Ontario L2A 5X3

Want to try two free books from another line?
Call 1-800-873-8635 or visit www.ReaderService.com.

* Terms and prices subject to change without notice. Prices do not include applicable taxes. Sales tax applicable in N.Y. Canadian residents will be charged applicable taxes. Offer not valid in Quebec. This offer is limited to one order per household. Not valid for current subscribers to Harlequin Desire books. All orders subject to credit approval. Credit or debit balances in a customer's account(s) may be offset by any other outstanding balance owed by or to the customer. Please allow 4 to 6 weeks for delivery. Offer available while quantities last.

Your Privacy—The Harlequin® Reader Service is committed to protecting your privacy. Our Privacy Policy is available online at www.ReaderService.com or upon request from the Harlequin Reader Service.

We make a portion of our mailing list available to reputable third parties that offer products we believe may interest you. If you prefer that we not exchange your name with third parties, or if you wish to clarify or modify your communication preferences, please visit us at www.ReaderService.com/consumerschoice or write to us at Harlequin Reader Service Preference Service, P.O. Box 9062, Buffalo, NY 14269. Include your complete name and address.

HD13R